Total-E-Bound Publishing books by Elizabeth Lapthorne:

The Agency Volume One
Flirting With Danger
Courting Passion

The Agency Volume Two
Passionate Immunity
Passionate Vengeance

Wicked Teacher

I0663235

THE AGENCY
Volume Three

Intimate Knowledge

Unearthed Treasure

ELIZABETH
LAPTHORNE

The Agency Volume Three
ISBN # 978-1-78184-628-5
©Copyright Elizabeth Lapthorne 2013
Cover Art by Posh Gosh ©Copyright 2013
Interior text design by Claire Siemaszkiewicz
Total-E-Bound Publishing

INTIMATE KNOWLEDGE

Prologue

Jennifer Mabbot never did work out what the noise was that had grabbed her attention in the cool autumn evening. In hindsight it could have been a rustle the strange man had made, or the metallic clink of his shovel against a stray stone in the dirt, or perhaps just the primitive awareness of one human being in close proximity to another. In the end, it didn't matter. The simple fact was she had heard something, and curiosity had got the best of her.

She'd come to the Forest of Dean to do some soul-searching and rough camping. Jennifer wanted to confront herself, be removed from all the modern tools of distraction and procrastination. She needed quiet time, some space alone to straighten her head out and decide her priorities. Jennifer understood she needed to think about the direction her life should take over the coming few years.

Earlier in the evening, her thoughts had begun looping around themselves endlessly. A fierce determination to resolve her personal problems had turned from something she had felt confident in doing into a near overwhelming task. Her self-assurance had begun to waver. Before doubts had been able to creep in she'd decided to crawl into her heavily insulated sleeping bag and get an early night. Her issues would be clearer in the coming dawn, she felt certain.

But then the strange sound had intruded upon the silence of her evening.

Her heart pounded, the animalistic, instant response freezing her body. Jennifer grabbed the thin penlight she'd carefully laid beneath her pillow in case she'd needed the bathroom during the night. Extracting herself from her sleeping bag she pulled her sneakers, scarf, beanie and coat on. She left the tent, standing in the crisp, cold air, straining to listen.

The section of forest she occupied was deserted — or so she had believed — but still the silence was not absolute. Leaves rustled, the wind moved blades of grass and cars could be faintly heard a few miles away on the main road.

A grunt sounded.

Jennifer almost jumped out of her skin.

She pressed her hand to her mouth to still the shriek that tried to escape her lips. Turning around in a slow circle she took stock of her vicinity, her eyes long since having acclimatised to the darkness. The landscape was grassy but flat. In the absolute darkness of the evening, though, it was still treacherous. Trees and large rocks littered the surrounding area, providing the cover Jennifer had decided would be useful if the forecast rain should hit early.

This time the scrape was clear, the noise carrying through the air. Something rang through the air and the earthy thump of digging was unmistakable.

An avid reader, all sorts of scenarios flew though her mind. Having also watched a few too many late-night scary movies, particularly gory highlights from those also entered her brain. Vivid visions of mobsters burying bodies or axe murderers with bagged, dismembered limbs vied for attention in her brain.

Drawn forward despite the caution common sense screamed at her, Jennifer carefully stepped over the uneven ground. After a few hundred yards the noise was louder. Someone was definitely digging.

A shadow loomed in the darkness. Having made her way without the light, which was still in her coat pocket—worried it might draw attention—Jennifer huddled behind a tree, wrapped her arms around the trunk both for support and to prove to herself this was not a dream. Clinging to the rough bark she peered around, fairly certain she was hidden not only by the dark of the evening, but also the shadow created from the tree.

A slender man bent over the soil, his attention fully taken in the task he performed. He lifted a shovel, pushed it into the ground with his weight behind it and pressing his foot into the movement. It sank readily into the dirt. He continued to dig.

Frowning, Jennifer leaned around the tree, straining to search the man's surroundings. She could not see a body, or garbage bags, or indeed anything he might be trying to hide.

Relief warred with disappointment.

Bolder now, Jennifer moved quietly to stand beside the tree. She remained well hidden in the darkness and shadows cast from the forest, at least a hundred or more yards away from the small clearing.

She had an unfettered view of this stranger as he worked away, and she no longer cowered like a frightened child. The man was tall and of a slight build. He wore dark-coloured clothes, black or maybe grey. He breathed heavily, small puffs of mist escaping his mouth. He panted from exertion.

She watched as he knelt to the earth and brushed at the hole he'd created. He dropped the shovel to the ground, stood again and tossed his head back. Jennifer noticed he had longer hair than she'd first observed. It too was brown or perhaps black. It was long enough to touch his collar, but in the darkness his hair blended with the coat he wore, so she couldn't tell exactly how long it was. He lifted a pale hand to brush the strands away from his face, tucking them behind his ear.

Jennifer couldn't make out his features, but she could tell he was Caucasian. She also knew from his movements that he was definitely male and neither extremely young or old. After brushing his hair back and giving his head a shake he picked up a small backpack she hadn't seen in the gloom.

Virtually empty, the bag had lain almost flat on the ground and had been easily missed by her. The man cast a glance around him. Jennifer pressed her body back against the tree, her heart hammering as fear spiked through her once again. Even though he didn't notice her, he had to have looked right past her. Her skin crawled. She felt certain his gaze didn't pause on her, but fear made her almost dizzy. Tiny pin pricks stabbed the nape of her neck, and for a paranoid moment Jennifer thought she was being watched.

The man dug into the bag, clearly not worried or aware of her presence. But Jennifer glanced around her. Something triggered her instincts. The forest was empty except for herself and this stranger, no movement or noise indicated anything different. But still her mind insisted she was being observed. Heat and awareness jolted in her blood, and she struggled to inject some common sense into her mind.

Jennifer shook her head.

"You're paranoid," she whispered to herself. "Delusional and feeling guilty for spying. Snap out of it."

Not feeling able to leave at this late point, she returned her attention to the strange man. He had dropped the backpack to the ground again, but now held a wooden box. A little smaller than a shoe box it didn't appear particularly heavy as the man held it with a relaxed grip.

Kneeling, he placed the box in the hole and started moving dirt back in with his bare hands.

Quite disappointed, but eased by the seeming normalcy of the entire situation, Jennifer watched for a moment longer. Just as she was ready to leave, the man stood, brushed the dirt from his knees and picked up his backpack. He turned his back and started to move away. Satisfied that was it, she turned away. Slowly picking her way back towards her tent, she mulled the situation over.

She could easily think of a dozen and more reasons why someone would want to come into the forest to bury a small box. It could be his retirement fund, a secret stash of money, or small items he'd purchased to evade some tax. It could even be legitimate earnings the man just wanted to salt away so his wife didn't go on a shoe shopping binge. Or maybe it was private documents, proof of embezzlement or copies of legal forms he didn't want others knowing about. It could even be a few discs or memory sticks filled with a dirty porn collection. The list was endless.

Whatever it was, he'd buried it out there and it was none of her business. Walking faster now, caught somewhere between guilt for snooping and eagerness to return to her warm sleeping bag, Jennifer was ready to get back to her bed. As she came upon her small camp her skin prickled again, but this time it was enough to raise the hairs at the base of her neck.

She froze, ancient hunter-prey instinct taking over. Jennifer glanced around her, frowning as she tried to work out if her imagination had overheated or if maybe the man had seen or heard her leave and had followed her.

Nothing except those sounds she was now used to reached her. She couldn't see anything unusual. No strange shadows, no looming people, nothing. Her heart beat loudly, and there was a faint ringing echoed in her ears as her blood pounded. Jennifer tried to control her breathing, the urge to pant in fear strong enough to make her shake.

Seconds crept by. A clock ticked in her brain as she struggled to calm herself.

Nothing stirred.

Her gaze penetrated into the darkness but didn't reveal a thing.

"You're losing your mind," she chided herself, saying the words aloud so she didn't feel quite so vulnerable. "Getting paranoid, my girl. Going to be jumping at shadows and starting to weave conspiracy theories any moment now. You need a good night's sleep and maybe a shot of that whisky you brought along."

Muttering to herself further, she crouched and entered her tent. She toed off her shoes and stripped off her outer wear. Jennifer ran a hand through her long blonde hair, finger combing it before climbing back into her sleeping bag. Taking a few deep, even breaths she tried to calm the racing of her heart.

Determined to get some sleep, she snuggled down into the soft cushion of her bag. Jennifer focused on clearing her mind. A few minutes later, when her ears had picked up nothing but the natural sounds of the forest she relaxed properly.

Shortly after that, she fell into a deep, dreamless sleep.

Chapter One

A week or so later…

Jennifer rounded the corner and turned into her street. Her head bent low against the misty, drizzling rain, she tugged her beanie as far as it could go. Her ears were starting to freeze off. Focusing on her steps, she remained oblivious to the world around her, her attention focused on the long, steaming hot bath she planned to take the second she entered her flat.

Never had she been more grateful for a Friday. Despite the fact she'd only worked the last three days after returning from the Forest of Dean, she was exhausted, chilled to the bone and weary in a way she'd hoped to overcome on her short camping trip. She felt like she'd worked a full week, and considering the pile of still unfinished work she'd left behind, that just depressed her spirits even further.

A few doors down from her flat she tugged one glove off and dug it into an outside pocket of her work satchel. The strap was across her chest, the satchel itself resting against her upper thigh to make it more difficult for a random thief to snatch it from her. The bag was battered from years of use, but Jennifer didn't care, she loved this satchel. It had tons of pockets of all shapes and sizes. She kept an umbrella in one, her phone in another, pens and a notebook in case she had an idea—or a shopping list—to jot down in random moments, all sorts of paraphernalia secreted into its depths.

A smaller zippered compartment on the outside was perfect for holding her keys. It was this she undid and rummaged through, determined to not waste precious seconds standing on her front step in the cold. Jennifer had plans, big ones. First she'd start running the hot water. This would be quickly followed by stripping and putting on her worn, fluffy robe. Then a strong drink. Oh yeah. She deserved something decadent. Maybe a hot toddy?

Her mind full of these lovely thoughts, Jennifer kept her head down and her focus internal. She climbed up the stairs, keys in hand and entered her tiny flat. Instinct took over as she started ticking off the items on her mental to-do list. She dropped the keys in the bowl by the door and switched on the lights as she kicked the door closed behind her.

Without missing a beat she strode directly for the bathroom, still rugged up in her winter gear and wearing her satchel. She was halfway across her living room, heading for the hall and her awaiting bath when an enormous figure stepped out of the kitchen.

Jennifer screamed shrilly.

Well over six feet and heavily muscled in a powerful, weights-pumping manner, the thickset man grinned. It wasn't a pleasant thing, but an expression that made her stomach churn sickly.

"Well, lookee here, who's come home finally."

Jennifer froze, surprise overpowering her. She could see this man, but his presence didn't seem to want to compute in her brain.

"Aww, she's gone all shy," he continued as he scratched his ginger beard. His grin widened. "Well, I'm not too worried about that, I'm sure you'll be very verbal once I get to work on you."

Jennifer shook her head and took a shaking step back. She knew — or rather desperately hoped — in a second or so she'd turn into some sort of superhero. Part of her mind envisaged herself fighting this man, beating him senseless and fleeing, but her body refused to do anything but quiver.

"What do you want?" she asked, struggling to hide the fear that threatened to overpower her completely. She flicked her gaze up and down him, trying to make sense of the situation. Her eyes were drawn to his heavy work-man's boots. They were cracked, worn and clearly well used. It was the most normal, least threatening thing for her brain to latch onto. It took a second, but she finally understood why that detail captured her attention. Those boots weren't what a regular thief would wear. They were thick-soled, clompy and noticeable. Coupled with the man's powerful physique it suggested to her that he was no ordinary thief.

Which meant he was there to hurt her, or worse.

Jennifer took another quick step back, her heart pounding harder.

"Now don't be like that," he mocked in his rough voice. "We're going to be great friends, you and I."

He strode across the room with a speed that belied his bulky body. Jennifer scurried back a few more paces but didn't make it to the door. He reached out a hand and clenched it tightly around her arm, hurting her even through her bulky coat.

Gasping and unable to draw oxygen into her lungs, Jennifer looked wildly around her for a weapon or anything useable. Her panic seemed to deepen the man's amusement.

"I'll tell you a secret," he said in a low tone. He leant forward, his pale eyes glowing with humour, or maybe pleasure. The thought that this man enjoyed capturing her, hurting her and scaring her silly made Jennifer shudder. Her fear ratcheted up another notch. She felt violently unwell.

"I hope you don't tell me where it is," he continued. "I can't wait to hear you scream, to make you cry so loud you think you'll burst. I love it when they give me pretty ladies like you. Especially when they tell me to take my time and do it right. I once had someone hold out for four days on me. She told me what I needed to hear, though, they all do eventually. I have something special planned for you, oh yeah. You're going to scream, Jennifer Mabbot, for me and because of me, that's a promise."

It was impossible to ignore his breath. It was fetid. Jennifer turned her head away, both from the rank, sour smell and his words. She had no idea what was going on—it surely had to be a mistake? But then why did he know her name?

Her entire body started shaking. Jennifer drew in a deep breath—about to scream bloody murder in the hopes one of her neighbours would hear, the walls were notoriously thin—but Ginger seemed to know exactly what she was going to do. He brought his other hand around her throat, tight.

"Now, now, Jenny," he murmured. He pressed her back into the wall, his own body hard against hers. He was rock-solid, clearly enjoying this, and thickly erect. "Let's not get the party started too early."

Jennifer struggled to breathe, her airways closed off by the man's large fist. She shuddered, her head spun and for a moment she wondered if she was about to die. The room whirled around her, her vision narrowing until all she could see was Ginger's face, the wiry, crooked hairs of his beard and the large pores of his skin.

"Don't kill her yet, you eager fuck," came a deep voice, seemingly from far, far away.

Her assailant loosened his grip around her neck, but didn't release her.

Jennifer's eyes fluttered shut. She choked, coughed. The action rattled her chest. Her body craved oxygen.

Focused solely on getting air into her lungs, Jennifer missed what Ginger said in reply. She forced her eyes open and struggled to look upon the second man who had entered the room. He wasn't as tall as Ginger and nowhere near as brawny, but still sleekly muscled in the manner of a man who works out religiously. Blond hair cut close to his scalp, he could have passed for an army man.

He wore thick leather gloves and held a sheaf of papers. A gun was lodged into the waistband of his jeans near his hip. His eyes were the coldest she had ever seen. Jennifer knew without the least doubt this man was a killer.

Remorseless.

Merciless.

She had to get out of here. Right now. Helplessness beat at her, but she forced herself to pay attention. She'd only get one chance to escape and it needed to be soon, but for that she'd have to concentrate.

"...I haven't found it yet but I still need a few minutes," the killer told Ginger. "Keep her occupied. Ask her some questions. That's why they hired you after all. Just be ready to move in a few minutes, we have no idea who else she might have spoken to."

Jennifer had no clue what he meant, or referred to. They obviously thought she had...something...and she doubted it was the new hardback book she'd bought the other day or her mother's pearls. It was almost as if she'd entered her home and had stepped into some other universe. Was everyone absolutely crazy?

The second man turned and strode off in the direction of her bedroom and bathroom. Jennifer huffed out a hysterical bubble of laughter. *So much for a relaxing soak in the tub.*

Ginger grinned—an extremely unpleasant sight—and roamed his hands over her body, attempting to remove her satchel and coat.

Her heart sped up again. The thought of having this man remove even her outer layers was enough to instil fierce panic in her. She knew she didn't have a hope against two of them, but one on one and with the element of surprise, she at least had a fighting chance. She tried to push him away, struggling as they grappled together.

Ginger grunted and appeared to enjoy the byplay. His breathing quickened. A light flush of arousal stained his cheeks.

While he was occupied Jennifer decided it was time to go for broke. She took a hasty breath and before he could react she screamed, "Help!"

Ginger snapped his head up, his eyes blazing.

Next door, her neighbour's large dog, Max, began to bark. It was a deep, ferocious sound and captured

Ginger's attention. With the thin walls and the volume of Max's barks it was impossible for Ginger to know where, exactly, the dog was.

Jennifer seized the few precious seconds of confusion. She reached down towards the small table she kept at the entryway. It held a small lamp and the bowl she'd drop her keys in each night. She grabbed the lamp and swung it hard against Ginger's head.

She'd hoped the blow would knock Ginger out, but she wasn't that lucky. His hands froze, his eyes wide and blinking as he tried to gather himself. She used that moment of stunned amazement to whirl around, jerk open her door and flee as if the hounds of hell were at her feet.

There were no shouts, and no gunshots. It was strange. She expected fireworks, the boom of cannon fire or at the least a raucous barrage of yelling and an enormous fuss. She risked a quick glance over her shoulder as she ran down her street.

Looking angry as hell, Ginger raced after her.

Adrenaline surged again. Jennifer shrieked and ran as fast as she could manage. The icy sleet had made the pavement slippery and dangerous to navigate. Panting, she turned out of her street, rounding the corner in a flurry as she tried to keep herself upright.

Falling, she knew, would mean instant capture. She didn't want to even contemplate what that would lead to. Ginger had made his intentions pretty clear, and Jennifer didn't doubt his partner would also be singularly displeased with the mess she'd created for them.

Jennifer glanced around her neighbourhood and struggled to think of where she could lose her attacker. It wasn't very late, but there wasn't enough foot traffic on the streets to lose him in a crowd. With only a brief glance for oncoming cars she raced across the road and headed towards a small market. As it was after working hours a number of the stalls would be closed, but many would still be open for the dinner crowd.

Dodging between the small groups of couples, most walking hand in hand and thoroughly dressed to combat the cold, Jennifer finally risked another glance behind her. She gasped, her heart hammering wildly. Ginger had fallen back but was still in pursuit. He had his mobile phone out now and talking into it. Certain her lungs would explode, she panted and somehow managed to keep up her pace.

Still terrified, but cheered that her attackers weren't superhuman, she wound her way farther into the maze of stalls and booths. Every chance she got Jennifer made turns at random.

After a dizzying number of twists, turns and back-tracking, Jennifer couldn't spot Ginger anywhere behind her. Walking around to the side of a stall, she decided to pause. Jennifer crouched low, wrapped her shaking arms around her knees, hugging herself tightly as she trembled.

Trying to breathe as quietly as possible, she let the panic wash over her.

What the hell was she going to do? What was going on?

Her world had turned utterly insane in the space of less than an hour. She certainly couldn't go back home. Should she call the police? But what could she say? That two men had broken into her flat and had threatened her? She had no idea what they were after or what this could possibly be in relation to. She was nobody, an ordinary, even dull thirty-something-year-old woman. As bland and non-descript as any other random woman on the street.

Determined to not crouch there cowering for much longer, Jennifer dug into her satchel, pleased she'd been too focused on her bath to get out of her warm clothes or drop her bag. She pulled out her mobile phone and paused. She needed to think for a moment.

Part of her mind urged her to call the police and push this whole mess over onto them. Simultaneously, however, a smaller part urged her to turn to the one man she knew she could trust implicitly. Pressing the numbers from memory, she called her childhood friend.

Saul Haslen and she had met back in the third year of primary school. He had protected her from playground bullies and she had been the only person who could always make him laugh. Tall, dark skinned and always on the outside the "cool group", Saul had insisted he loved how normal she was, and the peace and security her friendship offered to him.

Jennifer wasn't exactly sure what it was that Saul did, but she knew he travelled often, that it was covered under the elusive heading of 'government work' and that he was very, very good at it. Every now and then he'd give her a tiny titbit at their regular catch-ups, whether it was an anecdote from some exotic country he'd been in, or a joke his co-workers had shared, or even something Saul himself had witnessed.

Obviously she was in trouble. She needed someone to help her and watch her back. She trusted no one more than Saul.

Her hand trembled as she held the phone to her ear.

The ringing seemed to drag on forever. Her heart still raced and she kept checking around her in a twitchy manner she loathed.

"If you're calling to cancel our dinner tomorrow night I might just have to hunt you down and kill you, Jenn," his deep voice boomed from the other end of the line.

She hadn't realised how tense she was until the sound of Saul's voice had her muscles unclenching. All her stress had fled as soon as she'd heard her friend's words. Jennifer had no idea where Saul was — he could be around the corner somewhere in London or on the other side of the world doing secret stuff down in Australia. Regardless, merely connecting with him like this, hearing his voice made her feel a million times better.

"Saul?" Her voice hitched and the reality of what had happened came crashing over her. Tears filled her eyes and she didn't dare speak another word as she tried to get her emotions under control.

That single word seemed to be enough, however. He read everything he needed to in her simply speaking his name.

"What is it? Jenn, where are you?" he snapped out.

Jennifer knew he wasn't mad with her, she heard the worry and imminent panic in his voice. The only other time she'd felt like this had been when a blind date had turned disastrously wrong. Jennifer had called him from fifty miles outside the city, stranded and needing to be rescued.

She'd thought it would never happen again. Evidently she had been wrong.

"I'm at the market, around the corner from my flat," she spoke quickly and in a low tone. Her voice trembled, but as she spoke it all flowed out of her like a rotten poison.

"I couldn't think how else to lose Ginger. Oh, Saul, I'm in so much trouble and I don't even know why. They were just there when I got home, waiting for me, though I'm certain the killer was looking for something. I don't dare go back in case they're still there—"

"Wait, babe, slow down." Saul's voice soothed her, his words calming. She heard faintly the sound of his footsteps as he walked somewhere. "Start at the beginning. You're at the market, I got that. I'm heading to my car and I can be there in fifteen minutes. Now. What's going on? Who's Ginger and this killer?"

"I have no idea who either man is. They weren't exactly in a rush to introduce themselves to me. When I got home tonight they were already in my flat waiting for me. Ginger, I gather, was going to question me about where 'it' is—I have no idea what he's talking about—and the killer was farther back, probably ransacking my flat looking for this thing. Ginger..." her voice hitched again. Jennifer took another breath. "He said he would make me scream, Saul. He was excited by it, enjoying the thought of what his plans were... I'm really scared."

"And this man followed you?"

Quickly she explained how she'd escaped and now hid in the market.

"You can't stay there, babe. If Ginger was on the phone he's almost certainly bringing in reinforcements. They'll comb the area and flush you out."

Jennifer heard Saul's car start, the engine revving as he gunned it.

"Can you make it to Mel's café? She should still be open at this time, right?"

Jennifer nodded, understanding where she thought Saul was leading with his question.

"You want me to wait with her?"

"No, I was thinking she's on the edge of the market. She should also have access to the cellars underneath. You should be able to work your way under the street, to the loading dock in the alley opposite the area. It's the most discreet way for you to get out of there and hopefully escape the net these guys will be setting up."

"Oh, sure, I should be able to do that." Jennifer slowly stood. She stuck her head around the corner of the stall, taking a full minute to scan her surroundings and be certain she didn't see Ginger or anyone else looking focused, angry or as if they were searching for her in the vicinity.

"Jenn, you need to be careful—"

"I know. I'm taking this really seriously, believe me."

She didn't raise her voice as she headed for the café. Heart pounding, she wondered why she hadn't thought of hiding there herself. She regularly spent a lazy Sunday morning reading the paper and sipping hot chocolate at Mel's. Their friendship was superficial, but genuine.

"Where should I meet you?" Jennifer asked, more to keep her mind off her fear of being caught. "How about Hyde park? It's huge, we can easily hide there as long as you need."

"It'd be too easy to be followed there. Not to mention it will be practically deserted in an hour. No, I'll meet you at Buckingham Palace. You can easily catch the Underground there. Friday night, even in this miserable weather, there should be crowds for us to get lost in. Remember where we had that picnic and then hosted the treasure hunt for Sydney's birthday a few years ago?"

Jennifer wondered why Saul spoke in such a roundabout manner, but she knew the section of the Royal Parks he referred to. One of their mutual friends had requested a scavenger style treasure hunt for his thirtieth birthday party. She and Saul had put together a large part of the list and had a ball organising it.

"Yes. Saul…" Her words trailed off as she wondered what and how much she should say. If Saul didn't want to go into details over the phone, surely she shouldn't ask about it or draw attention?

Paranoia crept up on her. She glanced around, her gaze fearful as she studied the people that were around her. Jennifer hated this feeling, the jitters creeping back into her every action.

"It'll be okay," Saul soothed. "I'll see you there, Jenn, very soon, I promise. I'll help you sort this out."

"But…but how? Saul, I have no idea of what's going on. How can we fix something if we don't understand it?"

"One thing will lead to another. That's how these things go. We'll catch a hold of one thread, give it a pull and after a time we'll be holding enough threads the entire thing will unravel."

Jenn sucked her lower lip into her mouth, nervously grazing it with her teeth. A tiny part of her wondered if she should drag her best friend into this mess with her, but selfishly she wanted his help, his comfort and support.

"Jenn, do you trust me?"

Saul's voice was low, soft. Jennifer sighed. Just the sound of him soothed her and offered her the strength and comfort she so desperately needed. Warmth suffused her, the certain, rock-solid knowledge this man would do everything to protect and help her. Never had she loved him as much as she did right then.

"I do. Completely."

"Then we'll be just fine," he finished.

Jennifer smiled. She could hear the grin in his words.

"I'm glad you called me, babe. I'm relieved you turned to me."

"There's no one I trust or…can depend on more. You know that."

Jenn shook her head, annoyed with herself. She'd almost said 'love more'. A few times over the years they'd both come dangerously close to expressing more than just friendship to one another. One or the other had always backed off at the last moment. Jennifer wasn't sure why Saul had never explained his emotions fully, but for her part the thought of losing his friendship was enough to send her on a downward spiral.

She couldn't imagine her life without Saul. If that meant they remained friends and not lovers, then so be it. One of the things she'd needed to decide in the Forest of Dean was whether she should more actively seek love, open herself to new possibilities.

"You should be close to Mel, now," Saul spoke a little gruffly, breaking into her thoughts.

"I'm nearly there. I can see her front door. The lights are still on and there's people sitting inside."

"Okay, hang up and call me again the minute you're out and on the street again. I don't want you distracted, talking to me or anyone else for this. You need to be focused completely on your surroundings. And don't drop or lose the phone, no matter what."

Jennifer grinned. Saul's voice snapped with command, his tone urgent. She understood though, he was worried for her.

"I promise. I'm going to hang up now or you might bite my nose off. I'll call back in a few minutes."

"I'll bite something off, that's for sure," Saul replied darkly.

Jennifer's breath caught. Often they would bicker or tease back and forth, but this felt different. Something had changed between them. Excitement and nerves flickered in her chest. Something deep in his voice brought her body to life. Her nipples and clit sang with it.

She wondered if the adrenaline of the fight, her flight, hiding and now imminent escape had heightened the gentle sexual teasing between them. Or maybe something really had changed from Saul's point of view. She didn't know, but an intrigued part of her looked forward to finding out.

"You don't scare me, Saul," she replied. Jennifer had meant to sound firm, confident, but even she could hear the faint hint of questioning in her voice. "You'd never hurt me, or bite something off."

"I'd never hurt you, no, babe. That doesn't mean I won't bite you. Call me when you get out and I'll see you soon in the Gardens. Now, hang up."

Feeling equally turned on and confused, she mumbled out an "okay" and pressed the button to end the call. This time instead of placing it in her satchel, mindful of Saul's admonishment not to lose it under any circumstances, she placed it in the back pocket of her jeans.

Her world still felt as if the very axis of it had changed, shifted somehow. Now, having contacted Saul and knowing he would be beside her soon, protecting her and helping her, she no longer felt anywhere near the same level of stress or fear. Oh, she was still scared—Ginger, the killer and any number of people after her blood still roamed the streets, searching for her. But with Saul on her side she felt safer and more confident of her chances.

Saul had never let her down. Ever. She doubted he would start now.

Though, something clearly was changing between them. She'd loved him for years, been attracted to him since their teens. That tone in his voice, that darkly sensual promise. She'd never heard it before—or maybe just never noticed it.

Opening the door to Mel's café, Jennifer glanced at the patrons quickly as she entered. It took considerable effort, but she focused on her surroundings, watching for something that felt off or someone paying too much attention to her. Nothing struck her as odd, so she headed for the counter, a smile and greeting on her lips for Mel.

"Hey there," Mel said cheerily. "You need a Friday night hot chocolate? The double choc-chip cookies are still warm from the oven, they're the last batch of the day."

"Actually, I need a huge favour." Jennifer leaned into the counter, lowering her voice so only Mel could hear her. "I know this sounds crazy, but I think there's a strange guy following me. I've spotted him a few times while I was browsing, and no matter where I turn he's just there, watching me and giving me the creeps."

"Do you need me to call the cops?" Mel said quietly, scanning behind Jennifer.

Jenn shook her head. "No, I've called a friend. I just want to use your back exit, leave without this guy being able to see me. Would that be okay?"

"Are you certain you'll be safe? There's always a few coppers hanging around the outskirts in case tourists get lost or can't find a taxi easily once it gets dark."

Jennifer smiled, pleased by Mel's genuine sympathy. "I promise. Saul and I are meeting just a short distance away, he's already in the car and won't be more than a few minutes. I just don't want to go back out the front, not while this man might be watching."

"Come on around." Mel lifted a partition of the smooth wooden counter and after throwing a quick look over her shoulder, Jennifer followed Mel around the back.

"Promise me you'll call the police if this doesn't work and that idiot finds you," Mel insisted as she unbolted the back door.

It creaked as it opened, showing a direct line into the alley as Saul had guessed. Jennifer hugged Mel in a quick but warm embrace.

"I swear. I'm not playing the intrepid heroine here, I'm a little embarrassed how freaked out I am to be honest."

"Swing by in the next day or two," Mel said. "Make sure you let me know this has turned out okay."

Jennifer promised, then looked carefully around the cobbled street. Taking a deep breath she hurried out, scanning the area with a paranoid intensity she'd have never believed possible earlier. Although she focused on her surroundings, a part of her mind still chewed on the riddle of her best friend and mulled over the possibilities their earlier conversation seemed to have opened up.

Chapter Two

Jennifer struggled to not pace. She stood on the grass at the edge of the lake next to one of the winding footpaths running through the Gardens near Buckingham Palace. Tourists came even at this hour to see the Royal Mews, the Palace gates and to peer into the well-lit windows of the Queen's Gallery. She checked her watch for the third time in less than two minutes. How could it possibly creep by so slowly?

A couple strolled closer, their arms entwined, the woman pointing excitedly to a fork in the path.

"That's it, over there," she said in what sounded like an American accent.

Jennifer noticed the man held a crumpled tourist map, one the popular hotels kept by the thousand. The couple moved with purpose now, practically ignoring her. Only after they'd passed did her heart rate climb down from the near-apoplectic fit they'd induced.

She really needed to get a grip of herself. Saul would be there soon. He'd promised her he was already on his way so she couldn't have gained that much speed on him using the Underground.

Pulling her beanie down over her ears, she wished for a moment she had a compact or hand mirror. She must look a wreck. Patting her hair, then fiddling with her scarf she kept a close eye on the people who wandered by. Various street lights cast orange and yellow glows along the footpath. The sound of traffic was close, though out of sight in the mammoth gardens.

Jennifer wrapped her arms around herself and tried to not let her nerves betray her.

"Jenn!"

Whirling around, she caught sight of Saul heading towards her. Relief crashed through her, almost strong enough to have her knees wobbling.

"Saul!" she called out, racing to him.

He grinned widely, his teeth flashing white against his dark skin. Black eyes seared into her and never had he looked as large, solid or safe as in that moment. Jennifer threw her arms around him, embracing him fiercely, clinging as if she never wanted to let go.

Saul returned the embrace and they stood melded to each other for a long minute. Warmth seeped through her chest. Jennifer wanted to think her friend imparted the heat from his own body, though she knew it was likely just the adrenaline and overwhelming feeling of security he radiated that heated her. Saul's arms were strong, thickly muscled and steady as a rock around her body. He lifted her slightly off the ground and she chuckled, tempted to wrap her legs around him and cling like a barnacle.

"I've got you," he murmured against her hair.

She tightened her hold and buried her face in the crook of his neck where it met his shoulder.

"You must be freezing, you're not dressed for this," she mumbled next to his soft skin.

Saul wore thin, black suit trousers and a long-sleeved shirt with a thin red tie. A scarf was tied around his neck, but was too short to be a man's item. "You stole that scarf from some poor, unsuspecting female, didn't you?" she teased him.

"A lady wants to throw her scarf at me, it would be ungallant for me to refuse," he said, laughing.

Jennifer chuckled and loosened her hold on him, only stepping a few inches away, leaving their arms linked together.

"Plenty of ladies throw far more than their scarf at you," she replied. "It doesn't look like something you'd buy yourself."

Saul was sinfully handsome, and not just because of his sleek, muscular physique. His shaved head gleamed in the glow from the lamps. His eyes were frequently alight with laughter and mischief. And his grin...that wicked, knowing smile would have a bashful virgin shimmying out of her white cotton knickers faster than a regular bloke could snap his fingers.

He oozed a friendly, rough-and-tumble sex appeal that most women found enticing and addictive. He turned those dark eyes onto her and Jennifer found something low in her stomach unfurling, heat wrapping its way up to her chest while simultaneously her clit throbbed with the desire to be stroked.

Saul took her hand in his, laced their fingers together and pressed a warm kiss to her knuckles.

"I borrowed it from a co-worker," he said.

Jennifer blinked, having lost the thread of the conversation. Oh yes, the scarf. Looking around them, she realised for the last few minutes she hadn't even thought about the men who had tried to kidnap her, hurt her. Just being with Saul had already given her peace of mind.

"We should get out of here," she insisted, fear creeping back into her words. Jennifer glanced around. A part of her worried, but now he was here it was too late to focus on that. "I don't want you out here, exposed if they find me. Maybe we should—"

"We're safer here in the park, where we can see them coming," Saul insisted, though his tone was kind. "I'll be fine for a while, let's go and sit over here on the grass and you can tell me everything."

Jennifer frowned, though she didn't resist when Saul led her away from the path and into the gardens proper. He found a tree with a wide, flat radius of grass beneath it, presumably where he could see anyone coming towards them. He circled the tree slowly. Saul's gaze roamed over the area with an intensity that made her think he scouted for ambush points. Seeming satisfied with a particular spot, he leaned against the tree, drew her up to his body and wrapped his arms around her in a protective and defensive manner.

"Okay, babe, what's happened?"

The events of the last few hours come crashing down on her. Tears threatened to fall. She gulped, determined to not bawl like a baby.

"I don't even know where to start," she said, feeling helpless.

"Just go over everything in order. Begin from when you walked up to your door after work this evening," he replied patiently.

Jennifer nodded, took a deep breath, then as calmly as she could manage began to repeat—again—the bizarre and terrifying events of earlier.

Saul had always admired Jennifer's courage. Always. At school one of the jealous girls in her class had spread a nasty rumour about Jennifer and how she was easy with sexual favours. The entire story was rubbish, of course, but even back then she had been a beautiful girl, blossoming into a stunning woman.

Her long, honey-blonde hair had a faint curl to it— something he knew Jenn ruthlessly straightened every morning. Her warm blue-green eyes could reflect laughter and the inner joy she found in so much of the world around her, lit with an innocent happiness even back then, which Saul had cherished and loved. His response had been to want to pick a fight with the bitchy girl and punch her in her too-perfect nose.

Jennifer had held him back, rising above the whispers. Saul had shown her how to punch and defend herself. A few well-placed kicks to the groin and two broken noses later, a couple of men who had tried it on with her had at least learnt Jenn was not a loose woman and neither seduction nor coercion would be welcomed by her. The whispers had turned in another direction and life had moved on.

Yet he'd never forgotten the spirit and courage this woman showed ran right through to her core. She was stunning to him, and not just in the willowy, slender build of her body, the pert perfection of her breasts or the luscious softness of her long hair. Jenn had a purity of spirit he craved like a drug, and an optimism that had seen him through many a dangerous, depressing situation.

Knowing there were women like Jenn out there—innocent, happy, normal women—was one of the main reasons he'd joined The Agency. Fighting the good fight, trying to rid the world of evil and people who would happily destroy the very foundation of what Jenn believed in. Discovering Jenn being dragged into the shady nastiness of the world he inhabited scared Saul to the depths of his soul.

He listened carefully as Jenn outlined again the events as they had unfolded. A hot, angry flame of rage licked inside his heart as she repeated Ginger's words as best as she could recall them. Saul desperately wanted to find this man and tear strips of his flesh from his body—but that would only appease the fury within him for a short time. He needed to find the root of what had started these events.

Jenn looked at him, worry clear in her beautiful eyes. Saul reminded himself despite their long years of friendship and the fact he'd let her closer to his heart than any other woman alive, there was much of him Jenn didn't know of. He'd never confessed the true nature of his work—though he felt certain that was about to change very soon—but more importantly she had no idea of what his job entailed. The things he had done, would continue to do. She was not a part of his life in that manner. Neither did he want her aware of it.

He couldn't bear it if she looked at him with fear, or worse, revulsion. He was far from a saint, but he had always been the protector for her, the knight errant. Saul didn't want that to change. He teased Jenn that she was the only normal person he knew, and in so many ways that was the truth. More than that, though, when he was with her he could pretend—even for a short time—that he was normal as well. It was just another thing he cherished about his friendship with this woman.

"I know I probably should have called the police," Jenn said, finishing her story. "But...I don't know. I know you, I trust you. And if you think we should go to them, I will. But it's such habit, to turn to you for help, for protection. You were the only person I could think of to call and rely on without any questions."

Warmth crept from his chest up his neck. Saul smiled. He loved her with all his heart. He wrapped an arm around her shoulders, drawing her slender body into the safety of his own. He pressed a light kiss to the edge of her temple. A stray strand of her hair tickled his cheek.

"I'm glad you called me," he replied, his tone rumbling with emotions he struggled to contain. "I've told you often enough you can always call me, depend on me, no matter what the circumstance."

"Bet you're thinking I'm not so normal anymore," she joked.

He knew her well enough to understand, despite the attempt at jovial teasing, a lot of strain lay under her voice. He wrapped his other arm around her, hugging her tightly.

"You are still, far and away, the most normal person I know, Jenn. Never doubt that. You're an island of sanity in my crazy world. Believe it."

Jenn huffed out a disbelieving laugh and shook her head. She looked up at him, her gaze roaming his face, clearly expecting him to be teasing her or telling her pretty lies to make her feel better.

He met her eyes steadily, silently warning her they were getting dangerously close to truths he wasn't sure he wanted her to know. Despite the awfulness of her evening so far, this was not even close to the insane situations he'd often faced in his work.

His world could be insane, filled with terrorists and a level of paranoia high enough to send most people into an asylum. Locks and codes, encryptions and double dealings, not being able to trust anyone implicitly in case double speak backfired or other agents were listening in, industrial espionage and inter Agency in-fighting. All this wasn't even scratching the surface of the world he lived in. Saul had long ago built walls, impenetrable defences where nothing was taken at face value and everything was to be questioned. It was a reason he was one of the best agents around, and still here to tell the tale about it.

"You don't have some boring desk job working for Her Majesty, do you?" Jenn said in a soft tone, clearly reading some of the truth in his eyes, possibly for the first time.

He shook his head.

"I'm probably in deep shit here, aren't I?"

"I'm not sure, babe," he replied honestly. "Has anything strange happened around you lately? Any odd phone calls or people following you? It's possible someone connected to you through me, that this leads back to my door. If that's the truth then I will never be able to forgive myself, but it sounds like these men thought you had something, that you knew where this 'thing' they're searching for is. They weren't asking about me, or a person, but a thing. Think, Jenn. Is there anything weird that's happened lately?"

Jenn surprised him, and not for the first time this evening. She leant back against his chest, rested her head in the curve of his neck and frowned in thought. Her body pressed along his with an ease that startled him. They'd been friends forever, yes, but never physically intimate, or close in this manner. Hugs, kissing each other's cheeks, certainly. But never invading one another's personal space.

Saul found he liked the feel of her in his arms, pressed warmly into his body. He could become addicted to it, easily.

He wrapped his arms tighter around her, protectively but also relishing the solid reality of her in his embrace. She fitted there, so perfectly it was as if they were made for one another. He wished it hadn't taken them so long to reach this point. He burned to kiss her, to taste her lips under his. He itched to brush his hands over the smoothness of her skin.

Saul had seen her body enough times, swimming at the beach or in skimpy clothes mid-summer, to know what she looked like, but still his imagination took flight. He could all but feel what her skin would be like beneath his fingertips, taste the salty tang of her sweat on his tongue as he thrust his cock deeply inside her clenching, tight pussy. Her back would bend, her hair falling down onto his pillow as he pounded inside her, pushing her towards climax. She would press her head back, her neck arching as she screamed and —

"Saul?"

The worry in Jenn's tone snapped his attention back. She tilted her head up to search his face, her mouth turned in a small frown. She cupped his jaw, forcing him to look at her.

"Are you okay? What were you thinking?"

"I'm not sure you really want to know," he hedged. Desire ran him hard, but he couldn't find it in himself to deny her if she truly wanted to know. For years he'd wanted to confess his feelings, but had been reluctant to drag her into the misery and often destructiveness of his world.

Now she was here of her own volition, however, he couldn't find it in him to deny either of them much longer. Jenn's gaze searched his and she reached her thumb out to caress over his lips. His breath caught, his heart fluttered like a callow youth's. Desire had his shaft hardening. It would be all too easy for her to seduce him right there out in the public gardens, and to hell with the rest of England.

He pitied the poor fool who would try to hurt her. Saul would happily die to keep her safe, would undergo any risk, or perform any feat necessary to keep her whole. He cherished her above everything else. No one could hurt her or take her from him.

"I'm a big girl," she said. "I'm not afraid of you or your thoughts, Saul. I just feel...it's strange, but despite the fact we've known each other for most of our lives, it's like I'm seeing you for the first time tonight. Really seeing you."

"And what do you see?"

"A warrior, a protector, a hero," she replied even more softly now. She continued to touch his face, stroking his lip with her finger. "My hero. It's like you're every comic book super hero come to life right here for me now, to keep me safe and slay the dragon."

"I'm not like that, my world isn't like that, babe," he warned her.

She smiled, the reflection of light from the lampposts dancing in her eyes. "I don't know. You're always so hard on yourself."

Saul wanted to set her straight, to tell her — to show her — the truth behind the messy, grey, ambiguous reality of his world. His heart shattered into a million pieces, however. Jenn drew his face down to hers and kissed him passionately. He lost all reason, all thought. Everything blew up around him as he tasted her, the sweet intoxication of her lips and her taste as she slid her tongue into his mouth.

He'd fantasised for years about kissing this woman, knowing her in the most intimate manner possible. The reality was far, far better than even his most heated dreams. He groaned, caught up and utterly lost in bliss. Jenn had instigated the sensual caress, but Saul continued it.

He raised both his hands, then cupped her face, turned her slightly so he could press her against the thick trunk of the tree. He moved her back, then inserted his thigh between her legs. Jenn moaned — a soft, decadent sound filled with the dark promise of delicious sex. His desire enflamed further. Saul kissed her deeper.

They clashed their mouths together hungrily, each of them tasting and drinking from one another. He parried his tongue with hers, both vying for dominance in this intimate dance. Shifting his body, Saul made sure his larger frame would protect Jenn, shielding her from any prying eyes should they be unfortunate enough to be discovered by some tourists.

Saul lowered his hands and opened the top few buttons of Jenn's coat. Dodging the strap of her satchel and lifting her jumper, he finally found the soft flatness of her belly. The skin under the tips of his fingers was warm and soft, baby smooth and like a slice of paradise set before him.

Saul lifted his hand up under her shirt so he could cup her lacy, bra-clad breast. Heat seared his skin, branding him with her potent scent. She smelt of gardenias, a fragrance she'd always worn.

Jenn moaned again and moved her body against his. She shuddered as her thigh brushed over the thick erection pressing through the tent in his trousers.

When her hand touched him, even over the material of his trousers, he shook with the need to plunge inside her. He tilted his hips, moving his cock into her hand through his clothes. She stroked him, her fingers warm but agile.

"I need you," she panted, desire lacing her tone. "Saul, I'm burning up here. I need to feel you in me, please. Right now."

The faint sound of tittering laughter acted more powerfully on him than a bucket of ice water.

What the fuck was he doing?

Every instinct screamed at him. Years of training, all up in smoke from one potently intoxicating kiss from his best friend and the woman of his dreams. Not only had her small indiscretion negated his instinct, but it could also have signed both their death warrants.

Saul was not overly concerned with his own safety — he'd long since come to terms with the understanding that some day, sooner or later, his luck would run out—but far, far more importantly he'd put Jenn's life at risk. He loved her, needed her more than oxygen right now. But he'd rather slit his throat that endanger her.

He rolled them both so his large body covered hers. Pushing up onto his elbows, Saul breathed harshly, catching his breath and exerting an incredible amount of iron will to get his rampaging body back under control. He couldn't will his hard cock away, but he could bloody well get his mind back in the game and put his physical needs on hold until he had her safely locked away out of sight somewhere.

"Saul?" Jenn said, worry again in her tone.

"We can't do this here," he insisted huskily, lust thick in his voice. "You're not safe, and you're like a drug, or potent whisky going straight to my head. Much as I crave to be inside you right at this moment, fucking your brains out like I've wanted to for years, I won't risk your safety, not even for that."

"Like you've wanted to for years?" she repeated, sounding caught somewhere between amusement, amazement and a very female irritation.

Saul glanced at her, not quite sure why she was annoyed.

As if she could read his look, Jenn huffed and smoothed her shirt back down, buttoning her coat up again as she sat up.

"I've wanted you since we dirty danced at the party after we finished our finals at the end of Upper Sixth Form," she replied, clearly annoyed now. "But you treated me afterwards like your kid sister. If you dare tell me you've wanted me all this time and made me waste years—hell, more than a decade…"

Saul chuckled, stroked his fingers down her cheek. He pressed a hot but brief kiss on her lips.

"We can argue about that another time, babe. For now, we need to get you to safety."

"You know, I realise now you've never answered my question—when I asked what it is you do for a living," she chided him.

Saul set his clothes to rights and stood, holding a hand out for her.

"No, I haven't," he agreed with brutal honesty. "Maybe later tonight, much later, if you ask I'll answer as best I can. Then again, you haven't answered my question either, whether there's been something odd happen to you lately."

Jenn grinned, a warm, feminine, secretive grin that told of hidden truths, sexual satisfaction and every fantasy he'd ever harboured about or with her. It was a wicked, decadent grin that had his dick swelling even more in the too tight confines of his trousers.

"No, I haven't," she mimicked his words from a moment ago. "But maybe tonight, later tonight I'll answer your question, too."

He knew full well she wasn't talking about whatever was going on with her. The gleam in those beautiful eyes, the sexy tilt of her mouth and the sensual promise of her body as she pressed into him, against his side spoke volumes for what she really meant.

Whatever else happened tonight, the promise of what they'd started would be completed. He'd find satisfaction and Saul had every intention of fulfilling every single craving of hers as well. Saul touched his fingertips to her lips, stroking over the glossy smoothness of her lush mouth.

"Your protection and safety comes first," he said, more to remind himself than to reassure her. "I won't risk you, not for anyone or anything. Come on, babe, let's go before I lose control and just take you out here in front of God and every member of the public who cares to watch."

Jenn smirked but followed him without a word as he led them both out of the park.

Chapter Three

They were only a few streets away from Saul's townhouse when Jennifer finally recognised where he was taking her. For most of the drive she'd been wrapped in a blissful haze of fantasy mingled with reliving over and over the searing intensity of their potent kiss.

Their first real kiss.

Now she'd had a taste of him, Jennifer knew she'd never want to stop. She wanted more. Everything. Tiny thrills shot up her legs as Saul grazed her thigh with his large hand as he changed gears. After he'd touched her a few times she realised he wanted or needed the contact.

When he laid his palm on the gear stick she lightly rested her own hand over his. Warmth from his skin seeped into her. Her cheeks flushed, desire curling lazily in her stomach. Saul threaded his fingers through hers while they waited for the light to change. Neither needed to say a word, they both knew full well where this would lead.

Jennifer turned to watch this strong, dark man in the glowing lights reflected from the street. She'd known him forever, but at the same time she understood that tonight she was really seeing who he was. Although a part of her was scared of the situation, she couldn't help but feel grateful for the opportunity to really get to know every facet of him.

Saul turned. Their gazes met in silent understanding.

"Last chance to stop this," he said in a low tone.

Jennifer just grinned. Nothing, nothing in the whole world could convince her to stop right now. She wanted no more secrets. No more dodging or blurring of words, omissions or holding back.

Lifting her hand, she reached over to stroke his jaw. This small touch made her crave him. She shifted herself in the seat and leaned close to him, pressed her chest against the strength of his arm and tilted her head so she could kiss him fully on the lips. They fused their mouths together, heat exploding between them. Jennifer moved her lips, eagerly seeking more. She listed her hands higher, to stroke over the soft skin of his scalp, to massage her fingers down the length of his neck.

He moaned, as did she, need warring with common sense. Cramped and confined in the car, they would need some pretty impressive gymnastic skills. Tempted to move his seat back so she could climb into his lap, Jennifer weighed the loss of contact bending down to find the seat lever would require. But the payoff, to writhe in his lap, feel his hot cock resting against the curve of her arse would be worth it.

Before she could finish her thought and assemble her neurons into a plan of action, a sharp horn rent through the air. Saul snapped his head up, flickering his eyes up to the rear-view mirror, around the windows then finally back to her. He grinned, appearing almost sheepish.

"You're potent, babe. We're nearly at my place, give me just a few more minutes before you make me lose my head again, will you?"

Tyres squealed as Saul pulled away from the intersection. Although he kept their hands tightly clenched together, he no longer focused fully on her. Jennifer could see the small differences in her friend. His posture was more rigid, controlled. His gaze shifted constantly, searching the streets around them, checking his rear-view mirror and muttering "licence plates," presumably checking for vehicles that cropped up multiple times as they wove through the streets, turning left and right almost at random.

A dizzying number of turns later, they waited in an alley. Jennifer didn't need to be a genius to realise Saul was being absolutely, positively certain beyond all doubt that their tails were clean. Sometimes she'd teased him for being paranoid, over cautious, but now with this new understanding of what his job probably entailed, she couldn't fault him for his actions.

The mental picture of the dangers and hazards he fought against, the risks of his own life he put on the line constantly had her seeing Saul with new, clear eyes.

Saul finally pulled out of the alley and three turns later they were slowly cruising up his street. When he manoeuvred the car into an empty parking space on the side of the road, she turned to him with a firm stare.

"Those business trips you take, every two, maybe three months. They're not training courses and bigwig meetings like you led me to believe, are they?" she asked. Even she could hear the suspicion in her tone, though she wasn't angry in the least.

He grinned cheekily at her but didn't actually answer.

Saul opened his car door and came around to open hers. She climbed out and, shoulder to shoulder, they walked up to his front door.

"Later," he said.

There was so much meaning, a hot, sensual promise beneath the simple word it stole Jennifer's breath away.

She paused on the doorstep, surprised when Saul didn't immediately remove his keys and unlock the door. He bent low, his head almost level with her knees, and peered at the doorframe. Grunting, he then stood back up and rose onto his tiptoes, to peer in the top left-hand corner of the frame, near where the hinge would be.

A curt nod and he seemed satisfied by something.

Curious, Jennifer also moved low as Saul inserted his key into the lock. Before he opened the door, Saul pointed to a short, thin, single hair that had been taped across the doorway.

"Simple but effective," he said. "If anyone had opened the door, this would be broken, or moved. Doesn't mean the house is safe, but means a dumb-arse burglar or novice agent hasn't been in here during the day."

Not sure where to even begin responding to that comment, Jennifer pulled her satchel up over her head and shifted her weight, about to enter her friend's home. Oddly, he reached out a large palm and held her back.

"I need to check it first," he insisted. "I'll only be a minute. There are other safeguards in here. Jenn, if I shout out at you, even telling you it's all right and to come on in, run."

Jennifer frowned.

Saul leaned closer, took her chin with two fingers and tilted her head up so she stared him right in the eyes.

"If the bad guys are in here, they might try to force my hand, make me bring you inside. It's probably just that paranoia you so love to point out in me. But if I don't physically come out here, if I just call out, I want you to turn around and run."

"But where would I go?" she asked, fear creeping back into her veins.

Saul bent his head and kissed her, a light press of their lips, tantalising and teasing each other.

"I'll find you," he whispered the promise, darkly enticing. "No matter where you go, I'll always find you."

With that he dropped his hands and entered his home.

Jennifer remained behind on the front step. She shivered and for a moment thought she might be cold. But then she realised it was fear. She'd never understood how fear could blindside a person. It was like a living creature under her skin, prickling her senses, making her hair stand on end at her nape and acting like ice in her blood.

She hated the feeling.

The seconds crawled by. Time was the strangest thing. Since Saul had turned up at the gardens, the minutes had flown by. She'd felt secure, cherished, and horny as hell craving this big, wickedly delightful man. Now, even though he was only a few metres away from her, not being in his presence left her mind to roam into dangerous territory. She couldn't help herself, she worried maybe Saul's paranoia was all too real.

Straining to listen, she tried to detect if anyone else was inside the house. Her long-standing friendship with Saul was no secret. Had she truly brought danger to his door?

He's more than capable of taking care of himself, she reminded herself. Stomping her feet and wriggling her toes in her boots, she tried to inject some warmth from movement.

The hot, unpleasant feeling of being watched came over her again. Wrapping her arms protectively around her waist, Jennifer looked up and down the street, trying to see if anyone paid particular attention to her. Paranoia, she discovered, felt like a million tiny insect feet treading all over her skin.

Despite the street lights, much of the road was indiscernible in the evening darkness. A few lights shone in Saul's neighbours' windows, and a slow trickle of cars moved down the street—presumably people coming home after working late or heading out for dinner.

No one stood and stared at her. No one loitered casually smoking against a gate or post. Indeed, Jennifer couldn't spot a single soul. That almost scared her more than should someone be standing in plain sight, following her.

Footsteps sounded in front of her. Jennifer snapped her head around, only to see Saul coming down the hall, his grin infectious.

"It's fine, babe. Hey, are you all right?"

Saul wrapped an arm around her shoulders and she let herself be drawn flush against his body. Relaxing into him, she breathed in his clean, fresh scent and closed her eyes.

"I seem to just be freaking myself out," she confessed.

Jennifer breathed deeply and moved, putting a small amount of space between herself and Saul. A teasing comment sat on the tip of her tongue, something to try to lighten the moment and poke fun at herself, but she noticed Saul scanning his dark eyes up and down the street.

Professionalism was etched into his stony countenance, his body rigid with awareness. Doubt crept into her mind once again and she turned, letting her own gaze track around to see if anything struck her as odd or wrong.

"Looks like my condition is contagious," Saul said, a teasing lilt in his voice.

Jennifer frowned but didn't move her head. She felt the need to keep looking about her, making certain there was no danger. She didn't resist, however, when Saul gently used his arm across her shoulders to guide her inside.

"Wow, you must be worried," he continued. "You didn't use the chance to mock my paranoia and over-sensitive imagination. These men really have you scared, don't they?"

"I might be a little slow to start off," Jennifer replied. "But when I do get the message I can catch up quickly. Why did you let me tease you all these years? To a casual observation you might be a bit focused on people coming after you, but that's only because they have been tracking you. Your work is infinitely more dangerous than you'd led me to believe. Saul, I'm sorry."

He guided her through into the main living room. Jennifer dropped her satchel onto the couch, removed her beanie and scarf and started to unbutton her thick coat.

"Your teasing always reminded me that you were unconscious of any danger and completely innocent," Saul replied after a moment's careful thought. "You never mocked me or made me feel like a freak. Indeed, your acceptance and embracing of my perceived foibles, the gentle manner with which you teased me, it all added up to part of your charm, the thrall you held me in. There's no need, ever, for you to apologise for being who you are. If anyone should do that it's me. I never wanted to drag you into the seedy underbelly and infinite greyness of my world."

Jennifer shrugged out of her coat. Since she couldn't see a coat stand she let it drape over the back of the couch. With a warmth in her heart, she closed the distance between herself and Saul. Standing on tiptoes she pressed her body against his.

"Saul, no. You didn't drag me into anything. You've always been my rock, a solid, comforting presence in my life. Who else could I have possibly turned to when I needed help?"

"I don't want or need your gratitude, Jenn."

"I'm not offering gratitude, Saul," she countered with a wicked smile. Tilting her face up, she kept their lips a bare inch apart. "I'm offering me. All of me. In exchange for all of you. No secrets. No holding back. Everything."

Saul groaned but didn't say a word. He lowered his head and they kissed passionately. When he gasped she thrust her tongue between his lips, tasting him intimately. They twined their tongues and played together in an erotic game of parry-and-thrust. He closed his lips around her tongue, sucking. Jennifer melted into him. She moaned, heat pooling in her pussy as she grew slick, damp with need.

He chuckled, releasing her mouth again.

"Cheating," she panted. Catching his gaze with hers, she saw laughter in his dark depths.

He didn't respond to that, there was no need. Instead, Saul reached out and started to tug her woollen jumper up over her head. Eager, Jennifer let him and moved to start unknotting his tie and unbuttoning his work shirt. The sound of their laboured breathing filled the room.

Saul stole random kisses as parts of her body were exposed. An area of her belly peeked between the waistband of her trousers and the bottom of her linen top. With a speed and dexterity she sometimes forgot her friend held, he bent down, licked a slow swipe of his tongue over her naked skin, then pressed his lips to her hotly.

When she removed his shirt—the silky material flowing into a heap on the floor—Jennifer reached her hand out. She stroked the tips of her fingers over his warm, smooth muscles. Touching above his heart, she could feel the thumping of it. Such a strong, solid beat took her breath away.

Leaning close, she bent her head and kissed directly over the fast-pumping organ. Her imagination took flight, and she believed she could feel the rhythm, the beat of his life echo and reverberate through her lips. Saul stroked his hands over her skin as they slowly undressed each other. Jennifer felt almost as if she were captured in this perfect, beautiful moment in time.

Everything inside the room, inside her friend's whole house, appeared the same but completely different. Nothing had physically changed since she'd last been inside this very room, not more than a few weeks ago. The curtains, the rich, thick Oriental rug, the couch, the gorgeous landscape paintings hanging on the wall—everything was the same, but she perceived it all with new, different eyes.

Indeed, the only thing that had changed was Saul now stood before her bare-arsed naked, as she did for him.

His body was breathtaking, all hard, smooth planes, chiselled muscles and steely strength. She gazed at him, amazed this glorious man was about to be hers in every way. It wasn't just his physical beauty, she knew him so much deeper than that. He had the moral strength of a dozen men, a compassion she'd never been able to overlook or forget, and a fierce, almost primeval desire to protect those who needed it. That urge, as simple and instinctive as his name or skin colour, had been present from the day they'd first met. It was an integral part of his person, and one of the many reasons she had come to love him dearly.

In all their years together, she'd never seen his cock. Thick and long, standing proudly as it jutted out from his scrotum, it was a thing of beauty. She'd had a few lovers, none of whom she thought were as well endowed. Eager anticipation shot through her, her pussy wet with need and lust for this man's possession.

"Hell, babe, you're beautiful."

She smiled, wrapped her arms around his shoulders and—as she had craved to do in the park—jumped up and crossed her legs around his waist, rubbing herself along the length of his hard shaft. He carried her with ease, as if she were the lightest thing ever. It made her feel special.

"I was thinking the exact same thing about you, Saul."

They kissed again, eagerly exploring naked, warm skin. Saul palmed his hands around her arse, cupping her and stroking her flesh until she writhed with need, her lips slick from her own juices. Panting hard, Jennifer wanted this moment to last forever, but she needed to feel Saul inside her with a fiery intensity.

"Saul," she moaned. "Please. I need you."

She groaned as he moved a hand from her arse to dip into the pockets of his trousers where they'd been cast over the back of the couch. Trying to find coherent speech, Jennifer heard the crinkle of foil, answering her unspoken question.

She fluttered her eyes shut as Saul kissed her yet again. It took her a moment to realise he'd walked them both across the room. With the small square held between his fingers and both palms supporting her, he knelt on the thick rug. Carefully, as if she would break, he lowered her onto her back, his body settling comfortably above hers.

When the world tilted on its axis, Jennifer realised everything had changed, not just between the two of them, but in her universe. Nothing would ever be the same again. And surprisingly, she didn't care at all — she welcomed this change, the deepening intimacy between herself and Saul. She craved it.

She took the packet from him, ripped it open with her teeth and smoothed the latex over his shaft. He grew more in her hands, a slight thrust of his hips urging her to fist him, stroke him. Eagerly she followed his lead. Up and down she stroked his cock, loving the feel of him, the warmth emanating from his body.

Lifting her head she watched Saul, faintly disconcerted to find him staring at her, his gaze locked on her face. She smiled a little self-consciously.

"What?"

"You look like you're discovering a treasure, or maybe a secret."

She grinned, his words accurate. Stroking him further with one hand, she used the other to reach out and draw his head down to hers.

"I'm learning a whole host of new things. You're now my favourite subject to learn about."

They kissed again. Long, slow, drugging kisses that had heat seeping through her body, her moves becoming languid. His hands branded her skin, touching her, spiking her desire higher until she arched her back away from the floor. She pressed closer to his skin. Jennifer wished she could crawl up into him, become one with him.

A part of her craved to take her time, to explore his body with all his hidden, secret sweet spots, but the fire in her belly raged, her pussy clenching with the need to be filled, possessed.

"Last chance," Saul groaned hoarsely.

Jennifer shook her head, shifted on the rug so she could spread her legs wide open for him, splaying herself for anything he wished.

"This time we won't stop," she panted. "Not for anything."

Saul kissed her hard, his frame pressed down onto hers. They touched everywhere, stroking their fingers over deliciously naked skin, moving their lips over one another and tasting with their tongues. He lifted her thigh higher, the tips of his fingers sending thrills of pleasure across her skin. Jennifer loved the way Saul touched her. Reaching between their bodies she circled her fingers around the base of his cock, her thumb and forefinger barely able to circumnavigate his girth.

"Please," she pleaded. Guiding him to her pussy, Jennifer canted her hips. She looked up at him, watched as his eyes burned with hunger, drinking in the sight of her helping him reach her entrance.

He paused for a moment, his gaze flicking up to meet hers.

"I love you," he whispered.

The house around them was silent, the words seeming to reverberate between them. Jennifer gasped, the power and heartfelt meaning behind those three simple words cutting through her every defence and leaving her feeling raw, exposed.

He didn't give her a chance to reply. With a hard thrust Saul pushed the heated tip of his erection inside her. Jennifer's walls stretched, her pussy widen to swallow him whole. Slowly, but in a smooth motion, he breached her passage, pushing deeper and farther inside her.

"Oh," she moaned, the welling emotions rising with her, seeking an outlet.

Jennifer lifted her hands to clasp either side of Saul's waist. He took this as an invitation and pressed fully into her, his balls slapping lightly against her skin as he lodged into her as far as possible.

They both held still for a moment, locked their eyes together. Jennifer reached a hand out and stroked the pads of her fingers over Saul's smooth scalp. His eyes were black as pitch but filled with a wealth of emotion she couldn't begin to guess at. Despite the fact they remained quiet, breathing hard, she could still hear his words echoing around them, in her ears and seared permanently across her heart.

'I love you', he'd said, so simply, his emotions so bare and raw. There was no hiding here. No omissions or obfuscating the truth with a well-crafted story. The words were stark and potent, and had gripped her heart like a vice.

"I love you, too, Saul," she panted, her face flushed with heat, desire and an urgency she couldn't place. The words tumbled from her lips, inelegant compared to his admission, but just as heartfelt. "Always. Forever. I love you."

As if her admission had broken something inside him, Saul's eyes fluttered shut and he groaned deeply. For a moment she feared it had been the wrong thing to say, that something horrible had happened within him.

Then he clasped his hands over her hips, lifted her arse up and tilted her body for his possession. Pulling out of her, he then thrust back in one smooth motion, hard. Somehow it felt like he hit every nerve inside her passage with his thick cock, shooting sparks of current outwards and jolting her.

Her body came alive. Pleasure raced everywhere at once.

She gasped, unable to breathe from the overwhelming sensations.

In and out of her clenching pussy he plunged, gathering speed as sweat dotted his face. Jennifer clutched her hands at his back, seeking purchase she arched her spine up. The need to feel him closer, to push herself into him, grew inside her belly. Their skin became slick from perspiration as they came together faster and harder, their bodies slapped together as need overrode everything else.

"Saul," she panted, unable to articulate the blossoming emotions, the hard, near painful desire as it built swiftly and steadily.

"Jenn," he replied.

His gaze was serious, his face set in what she at first mistook for grim determination, but then realised he was exerting a mammoth control over himself.

"Take me," she panted. "Let it go, I can handle it."

Jennifer wasn't certain she could express herself even in the perfect circumstances, let alone half wild with lust as she was now. Saul seemed to guess or understand what she meant. They'd been friends forever, and now were far more than that. She didn't want or need him to pretend, to hold onto his control, to hide from her. She loved him. Accepted everything about him. She could take anything and everything he dished out and hoped to return it to him tenfold.

She cupped his face, sweating and not in the least self-conscious as she struggled to reach her climax. Saul roared and thrust within her, seeming to not just let go of his control but positively break free of it.

He bellowed, a dark, deep sound torn from his soul.

He pounded into her, the blurring pain so pleasurable Jennifer couldn't breathe. His huge shaft touched her inner nerves and her climax exploded within her. The room receded, reduced to the pinpoint of where Saul's cock possessed her cunt in its entirety. The world could have ended and she would have neither cared nor noticed. Only she and Saul existed in this perfect bubble of bliss.

Pleasure rocked her body, and Jennifer lost all her senses and didn't hear herself scream from the brutal climax. She convulsed, her pussy clenching around his shaft, milking him to within an inch of their lives. Her muscles spasmed, hungrily sucking every last iota he had to give her.

Like a wave crashing, Jennifer dropped from the highest peak she'd ever experienced back down to earth with an almost physical thump. If she'd been more metaphysically inclined she would almost have expressed it as if her spirit or soul had literally been cast high above her, and when her orgasm was finished she'd come back to her body with a snap.

Sweating, panting for breath and partially insensate, Jennifer opened her eyes to look around. Aside from the fact she viewed the room from the floor, she felt astonished to see nothing had changed. No earthquake had rent the apartment to rubble. No earth-shattering event had taken place.

Yet Saul shook above her, the final tremors of what appeared to be an equally vigorous climax still holding sway over his body. He shuddered, his skin had a sheen of dampness, his eyes wide from the force he had experienced.

Tenderly he withdrew from her then lay on his side next to her, taking his weight on one elbow. They stared at each other as if they were complete strangers. Jennifer smiled, silently reaching out a hand to cup her lover's jaw. She traced her thumb over his lips in a small, intimate gesture, not wanting to break the perfect silence of the moment.

He puckered his lips and pressed a light kiss to her knuckles, seeming as happy to enjoy this special feeling as she.

Shifting slightly, she pressed their lower bodies together, moving closer towards him as she basked in the afterglow.

Chapter Four

Jennifer drew the blankets up over her shoulder and snuggled herself both into the pillows and Saul's body. When they'd been capable of movement he'd stood, had held out a hand for her to take and had led her back to the bedroom. While she'd crawled into the large bed he'd quickly washed himself in the adjoining bathroom then had climbed in next to her.

Now, facing each other, they grinned sheepishly, like bashful virgins.

Wrapping an arm around Saul's waist, she drew their bodies flush. Jennifer tilted her head back a bit so she could look Saul directly in the eye. "I meant what I said earlier, about loving you. I'm nowhere near as pretty with words, like you are, but I wasn't speaking in the heat of the moment. I want you to know that, to never doubt it."

"For two people who have known one another as long as we have, I know we're going to learn so much more in the coming months and years," he said, his voice deep and husky.

Jennifer smiled. They idly stroked their hands over one another. She couldn't believe how wonderful it felt to be able to touch him at will, to feel his body naked and strong beneath her palm.

"Your job is really dangerous," she said after a few minutes of silence. "Isn't it?"

"Sometimes. At other times it's deadly boring. The amount of paperwork I often have to fill out boggles the mind."

She laughed.

"I'm struggling to imagine you sitting at a desk, typing out regular forms and arguing with the finance department. The image just doesn't suit you at all."

"Jenn, there are some things I can never tell you about—for your own safety as well as the fact I've signed a mountain of non-disclosure forms and gag agreements. But yes, the work I do for the government doesn't fall under the mundane label I usually lead people to believe. The Agency is caught in a grey area, somewhere between sanctioned and deniable, expendable and part of the glue that holds our world together."

"So all that travelling you've done over the years..." Jennifer chuckled and shook her head, understanding there was a line her questions could not cross. "No wonder you never showed me any pictures."

"Hey, I brought you back souvenirs when I could." He laughed.

She nodded, a small grin on her face.

"From now on, key rings and postcards won't cut it, Mister. I'm sure you can find odd knickknacks every now and then."

"Ah, so you love me for my worldliness? Good to know."

She laughed with him, enjoying the way they were both easing back into the comfortable familiarity of their friendship, but now so much deeper and richer than ever before. Jennifer traced her fingers over his head, stroking his skin tenderly.

"As long as you always come back to me, whole and well, I don't care where you go or what you have to do. The things you've probably done, the risks you so willingly take...didn't I tell you that you're a hero? You're even more than that to me now, but you'll always be the most amazing man to me, Saul."

"I'm not, Jenn, not even close. I know real heroes—I work with a number of them. I'm just...me. Paranoid and evasive. I don't rescue the innocents, I...protect other agents, shall we say. I watch our arses, second guess the enemy and make certain the team returns safe when I'm called on."

"A protector, a hero. A man you could rely on and trust with everything you hold dear," Jennifer surmised, feeling faintly smug. No, she hadn't seen this side to Saul. But every word he had uttered proved the man she had always cherished, the friend she had loved for years was exactly who she'd always known him to be.

Saul shook his head and wrapped an arm warmly around her waist. They faced each other. Jennifer scooted so closely that their bodies pressed together. Feeling more at peace than she could ever recall, Jennifer rested her head against his chest. The steady sound of his heartbeat beneath her ear made her feel drowsy.

Held securely in each other's embrace, they lay warm under the blankets for a few minutes, an easy, companionable silence between them.

"So do you know what set this all off?" Saul finally asked. "I'm happy to protect you forever, babe, but those men are still out there and sooner or later they'll want whatever it is they think you have."

"Mmm," she mumbled, having fallen into a light doze. "I'm not exactly sure, though I did think of one thing."

"What's that?"

"I went camping last week. I...wanted some time to get my head in order... I needed to do some soul-searching. Anyway, I stayed in the Forest of Dean, near those cabins we've rented a couple times over the years. You know, in the summer with Lu-lu, Mark and Tom. On the second night I was out there I woke up, there was a man digging, burying something in a small wooden box."

"A man...Jenn, and you didn't think this might be important?"

"I didn't get a particularly good look at him, but he was slim, with long hair. I know he was neither the killer and certainly not Ginger, so I didn't connect it at first. But it's the only unusual thing that's happened to me...well...ever really."

Saul frowned, his gaze wandering behind her shoulder as he thought.

Jennifer remained silent, letting him sift through what she'd told him.

"Why wouldn't they go to this man, if they want the contents of this box, why bring you into it?"

"What if they don't know this man stole the box?" Jenn guessed.

"Then how did they connect you to it? Indeed, I can't understand how they could have knowledge about you and not the box's location at all."

Seeing his point, Jennifer tried to make sense of the situation.

"I was there for a number of days after that night," she pointed out. "What if they couldn't get information about this man—or lost him in the woods and I was the only person they could find in the vicinity? My camp wasn't exactly a secret, I wasn't there to hide."

Saul raised his eyebrows, his eyes sparkling as he nodded and picked up the thread.

"If this man was savvy enough to ditch a tail—or even recognise he was being followed in the first place—then it's possible he's lying low, waiting for the heat to pass. That would follow with him wanting to bury whatever is in the box. If the people Ginger and the killer represent need the box, that doesn't explain why they didn't ambush you out in the forest, or why they waited so long to make a move."

"Maybe they searched for themselves first? And couldn't find where it was hidden. You know that area, it's huge."

Saul seemed to mull it over a bit longer. After a couple of minutes he turned back to her with a small smile.

She responded in kind, partly because his grin was infectious, but also because she understood his enjoyment of figuring out a puzzle.

"Do you think you could find the burial spot?" he asked.

She frowned, searched her memory.

"I could get us close," she guessed. "It was dark, the middle of the night. It also wasn't like I used a compass or map. I followed the sound of digging and someone working, it was just instinct, really random. But yeah, I could certainly take us near the spot."

Saul lifted his hand, brushed back the strands of hair that had fallen over her face. He did this tenderly, his mind clearly still struggling with the puzzle in his brain. She waited patiently, knowing he'd discuss it with her sooner or later.

"I don't like the thought of taking you back out there. It's a risk."

She huffed, both pleased by his protectiveness and frustrated by his treating her like a breakable object.

"There's no chance of you finding that buried box without me, Saul. The proverbial needle in a haystack doesn't even come close. And the box was wooden, I'm nearly positive. So a metal detector or sniffer dog wouldn't work either."

The grin he cast her was sheepish. Really, she'd been speaking rhetorically and maybe even a little facetiously. She hadn't realised until this moment he must have thought and discarded something very similar to just that. Shaking her head, she tightened her hold around his waist, squeezing him.

"We're a team, Saul. Equals. That's always been so between us. Now isn't any different. No, I'm not used to your world, and I'm sure you could tell me true stories that would have me running screaming. But I'm with you on this, all the way. And I will always support you. Always. If you try to ditch me I'll hunt you down and do nasty things to you."

"Nasty things?" he repeated, a wicked gleam in his eyes. "Do you promise?"

She laughed, the seriousness of a moment ago dispelled by his teasing.

"At the very least. Wicked and nasty things. Horrid, dirty, nasty things. It's an iron-clad promise."

"Well then, with the promise of horrid, dirty, nasty things that you can do to me — and at any time, babe —

tomorrow I think we'll both set off for the Forest of Dean."

"Then that leaves us with tonight," she purred cheekily.

Nudging one strong shoulder, Jennifer pressed Saul onto his back. He scooted down the mattress a little so his head rested on the pillow, his body open to hers. Her thigh brushed his leg as she moved to straddle him. She felt his cock twitch and start to thicken once again. She widened her legs and rubbed her damp pussy lips against the ridged plane of his flat stomach.

"About those wicked things," he whispered.

Jennifer pulled the blankets up around her shoulders to help ward off the chilly air, a small laugh escaping her mouth. Eagerly, she pounced upon him, bending down to steal his lips with her own. Kissing him ratcheted up the pounding of her heart. Desire and excitement vied for attention.

Bending lower, she whispered naughtily in his ear.

"I want to suck your cock deeply into my mouth, feel you fucking down my throat as you take your pleasure from me." She panted a little, her face flushing as she shared her fantasies. "Then, once you've come and you're slick from my mouth I want to know what it would be like to be possessed by you in my pussy and up my arse."

Saul drew in a breath, clearly struggling to maintain his control. The most delicious, powerful thrill raced through her. His hands were warm as they palmed her breasts and he lightly pinched her nipples. Pleasure shot through her body, her core dampened and her clit sang with the need to be stroked.

"Next time," he swore gruffly. "Top drawer."

It took a split second to understand what he'd meant by his second comment, but the sensual fog in her mind cleared. Sitting upright, then leaning all the way over to the bedside table, she tugged open the top drawer and removed a foil packet from the box. After sheathing him, she lowered a hand to tilt his thick, hot cock to the right angle.

Her eyes fluttered as she guided her body onto his shaft, the penetration deeper, more intense from this angle. Small trembles shook her body when she moved lower and lower. Full to bursting when she sat back against his wiry pubis, Jennifer shifted her weight slightly to ease the pressure of his possession. Gasping for breath, she groaned while Saul massaged her breasts.

He seemed to find a direct conduit between her sensitive nipples and the apex of her thighs. Her clit throbbed needily. Lowering her hand, she stroked herself with just the right pressure, hard enough to stimulate but not roughly enough to bruise.

"Ride me, babe," Saul groaned.

She'd never heard him plead like this. The heady feeling of power mingled with the lusty desire soaking into her body.

Obediently, she raised her body, then sank back onto his shaft. Nerves popped and liquid heat surged within her. Up and down she moved. Saul caressed her breasts in time to the strokes, and Jennifer stimulated her nub further. They danced together intimately, their bodies moving with a grace she'd never experienced.

Panting hard now, her second orgasm of the evening began to build long before she was ready to finish this.

"It's coming," she warned.

Instead of backing off, letting the moment draw out, he lifted his head and shoulders to capture one breast in his hot mouth. He sucked hard on her engorged nipple. The sweet sensation caused her to cry out. The pleasure intensified as she felt the hunger tug deep within her belly.

Bracing her free hand on his shoulder, pushing up with her knees and thighs, Jennifer rode Saul with a wild abandon she'd never known resided within her. She panted then shouted out. She pressed down upon him, thrusting onto his cock as hard as she could manage only to lift up high and repeat it over and over.

"Come for me," Saul pleaded, his eyes black as midnight. "Come hard, now."

Moving one of his hands, he placed his fingers over hers and stroked hard over her clit. The added stimulation pushed her onto the brink and she felt her soul fall. A small explosion detonated somewhere between her stomach and her pussy, pleasure rocketing outwards and encompassing her whole body.

Jennifer threw her head back and screamed her climax. Seconds later Saul thrust his hips up so hard he lifted her body from the mattress. His shaft spasmed and he shouted out, his pelvis pistoning at a rapid rate as he shivered through his own orgasm.

Grinding against each other, they came together, flesh slapping as they fell from the peak. Feeling shaky and wrung dry, Jennifer fell forward, her breasts pressing into Saul's chest. She buried her face beside his neck and into the pillow.

They caught their breath slowly, each recovering in their own time.

"If sex is always going to be like that between us," Saul said after a few minutes, "then I'm probably going to be dead of a heart attack within the year."

Jennifer chuckled but didn't have the mental coherency to answer just yet.

Saul gently pulled himself from her body and climbed from the bed. He moved into the direction of the bathroom and she heard water running. After taking a deep breath, she threw back the blankets and followed him, wanting to clean up before they fell asleep.

Saul handed her a washcloth. When they were both clean he held out his hand. She took it with a smile, trusting him fully.

He led her to bed.

With Saul's large frame wrapped protectively around her, Jennifer had never felt so complete, or as peaceful. She slept easily, her mind still subconsciously aware of Saul's warmth and comfort next to her. Her sleep was full of raunchy, wonderful dreams.

* * * *

David stood on the opposite side of the road, well down from the townhouse. He'd spent time walking around the surrounding streets, professionally scouting the area for the best vantage point. Pulling his scarf tighter around his neck, he subconsciously brushed the curtain of hair out of his face and tucked it behind his ear.

He had frequently thought about cutting—or at the very least trimming—his shoulder-length hair, but he'd never found the right time. The desire to get rid of it was moot, anyway. His co-worker and partner insisted he could disguise himself far more effectively with it long.

"It's the ultimate accessory. You can convincingly pass as anything from a bum on the street to some high-society knob of fashion," she'd insisted with a twinkle in her beautiful blue eyes. "Besides, I like the way it brushes your collar and falls like silk around your strong jaw. It makes you look... I'm fond of it like this."

David admitted only to himself it was her last point that had stayed his hand each and every time he was tempted to get rid of it. The way she'd looked at him when she had uttered those last words...yes. Soon he'd have to act on that. He knew it, and he felt certain she knew it too. Particularly with the thinly veiled looks of concern she'd been giving him lately.

A slight shake to his head dispersed all thoughts of his sexy colleague.

He focused back on the matter directly at hand. David knew he was in seriously deep shit. The woman had turned to a professional. He'd known from the moment he had felt her presence out in the woods that night that she was a loose cannon, the proverbial free radical and complete unknown.

Subjects like her turned up in his professional life very infrequently. Despite the madness, bloodshed and complete mayhem of his work, true unknowns were practically unheard of. Everyone had a past. If one had the patience and skill to dig deeply enough into the research facilities at his fingertips, usually even the knottiest of problems could be unravelled, studied, categorised and most importantly of all— neutralised—with very little effort.

Not even his heftiest of bribes and threats had unearthed the least intelligence on this woman.

That concerned him.

Deeply.

The last time he'd come across such an unknown, such a deeply buried past and uncontrollable woman, was when he'd partnered with her professionally — eighteen months ago. Even after all this time, while they knew volumes of information about each other, she still shocked and surprised him on a regular basis. He could accept that in his special lady. He could not, would not, accept it at this critical juncture in time from a total stranger.

David studied the townhouse, watching as the last of the lights were extinguished. He checked his watch, weighing his options and trying to carefully feel his way forward.

He now felt certain the woman had seen him, but was unable — or unwilling — to identify him. Since he'd felt her eyes on him as he'd buried that damn box he'd been confident she couldn't have seen him too closely, not enough for a positive, actionable ID. The simple fact her bodyguard hadn't spirited her into hiding — or worse, gone to the authorities — showed a small trickle of luck still flowed his way.

David calculated his plan of action with caution and precision. He needed to balance his own priorities with those of his mission and weigh it against the cost of what he was prepared to lose.

Eighteen months of work, more if he included the background and preparation.

When he thought of the situation in terms of what consequences he was willing to bear, one thing promptly became crystal clear. There was one item — one person — he was not, under any circumstances, prepared to risk. Not even under pain of torture or death.

Everyone—everything—else could go directly to hell as far as he was concerned. His top priority was his partner.

Suddenly, his decision and the path ahead of him seemed perfectly straightforward.

Reaching into the inner pocket of his pea coat, David removed a slim, tiny mobile phone. He flipped it open then hit the buttons without needing to look at them.

"Is everything all right?" a husky, sexy voice asked him drowsily.

David smiled. Should this be the first time he'd ever heard her voice he might assume he'd woken her from a luscious, highly erotic dream, her voice thick with sleep and promising darkly of sinful pleasure. He knew her far better than that, however. He knew this was how she always sounded, at least when she spoke with him.

"I might be compromised. We need to meet."

"Now? We're supposed to be incommunicado. Meeting wasn't in our plan."

Her tone was not dismissive—indeed, she sounded curious more than upset or unresponsive. David didn't look away from the townhouse. Mobile phones were notoriously poorly secured and he wanted to check no lights went on suddenly, indicating his line might be tapped. He also knew neither of them could go into details unless they were face to face. There was no other way to ensure both their secrecy and safety.

"Can I come to you?" he asked again.

There was a pause. David could almost hear her working out the odds, weighing her options just as he had moments earlier. "Always. I'll expect you soon."

Thick, hot satisfaction rolled through him when she finally answered, "Until then."

"Stay safe."

They disconnected simultaneously. David continued to gaze at the dwelling over the street, a new plan already forming in his head. Their timetable needed to be moved up. Feelers needed to be sent out to gauge other contacts' reactions to this woman's stumbling into something far greater than she could imagine in her wildest dreams.

David had nothing against her. A part of him wanted no harm to come to her, for she seemed like an innocent in all this.

He had a much larger plan in progress, however. More importantly, she wasn't his top priority. One thing he'd learnt in this game, everyone looked after their own interests. He wasn't as selfish as many, he had not fallen that low, but that didn't mean he was willing to risk his treasure for her either.

As he turned away, started back down the street to meet his lady, he hoped this woman's bodyguard—the large black man—loved her even half as much as he loved his partner.

Lifting his face up to the inky black sky, David breathed deeply, the icy air catching at the back of his throat. It was going to be a long night, a hard one. The knowledge he had someone by his side not matter what made him grin.

He wasn't alone. He had someone guarding his back.

They'd reconfigure their plan and with luck not drop any of the balls they juggled. Something he'd learnt well about his lady—she hated to lose and never gave up. It was one of the things that constantly gave him hope that one day they'd be more than co-workers. He wanted to be life-partners in full.

David doubled back and checked his tail. He'd been taught by the best, he had no fear anyone was as good as him. Tonight, however, he would use extra precautions.

The last thing he wanted was to bring danger to her door.

He only hoped the strange, innocent woman and her chosen bodyguard were competent enough to stay alive and see their way out of this mess.

Chapter Five

Jennifer focused on the narrow dirt track as she drove towards the clearing she'd used previously as her campsite.

"Right," Saul agreed as he spoke on his phone. "Yes, Preston, I think you should track him and his partner down. They could have information we need, or hell, they're obviously criminals. This is the sort of shit we're supposed to handle, right?"

Jennifer could see Saul rolling his eyes. She had to smother her giggles, knowing it was his boss he spoke to on his phone.

"Yes. You've mentioned that. And that. Okay, we're here, Preston. Look, I'll call you later."

Jennifer glanced to the side as Saul snapped his phone shut, ending the call.

"Is it wise to hang up on your boss?" she asked, more curious than concerned.

Saul shrugged and pocketed the small device. "I'm almost regretting going to him to try to track down Ginger and his mate."

"Earlier you said Preston didn't think he could use the description I gave? That is was too generic?"

Saul grimaced and cast her an apologetic look. "Preston got curious, asked around and ran the image we worked up through the Agency database. Ginger is actually called Vincent Daniels. That was what Preston's text was about and why I called him back just now. I'm hoping some of Vincent's known associates might turn out to be the other guy."

Jennifer digested this as she pulled up onto the edge of the small clearing. She switched off the engine and they sat in silence for a moment. Staring out of the windscreen and not seeing a thing, she decided if Saul or his colleagues could find her attackers, maybe even do something about them, then that would be perfect. Even having a name for Ginger made her feel scared still, but more in control.

"Thank you." She turned to face Saul. "If Preston or someone can find Vincent, then you're right. We can question him. Find out whatever the hell we've got into. Do you think…" She hesitated a moment, not wanting to burden Saul further but unable to stop herself now she'd started. "Do you think we can keep him off the streets? So he can't hurt anyone?"

Saul clenched his jaw. Jennifer huffed out a breath, something resembling a very weak laugh. Of course. She shouldn't have needed to ask. His gaze stayed with her, comforting her before he even opened his mouth to say a word.

"He won't ever hurt you, babe. No matter what. That's a promise."

She reached out and took his hand. Chemistry sizzled from the intimate contact.

"Thank you," she said again, softer this time, wishing she had more than just words.

Saul grinned, a sexy, wicked thing which lightened his features and made her heart stammer against her breasts. He opened the door with a jerky motion, squeezed her fingers again then climbed out.

The camp site, she recalled. The box. Right.

Blinking, she shook her head to try to clear her brain as she got out of the car. Saul stood to the side, his hands thrust deeply into his pockets. Jennifer glanced around and enjoyed the crisp air.

Déjà vu.

She turned a slow circle around the small clearing, mentally picking out how she'd set up her campsite the previous week.

"That's where I had my fire going." She pointed to a darkened circle. Even though she had carefully turned the ashes over multiple times in the dirt—pedantically making certain no stray embers could reignite after she'd left—the small area was clearly visible.

Saul knelt to the ground, his long fingers prying at a small hole in the earth.

"Tent pegs?" He chuckled. Now he'd drawn her attention to it, the half dozen small crevices leapt out at her. "Please don't tell me you're still using that ancient contraption from your childhood."

"Dad bought me that tent for my fifteenth birthday," she replied automatically, the argument an old one for them. "If I recall you snogged the hell out of Betsy Chandler in it during the summer break at the end of sixth form when the rest of us were off on a hike. I'd expect you to have even more sentimental attachment to it than I do."

Saul had looked up at her as she'd finished her comment, his grin wide and wicked.

"I'll buy you a new tent and snog the hell out of you in it, then. I fully intend to make a lifetime's worth of new memories with you, babe. Never doubt that."

She laughed and returned her attention to surveying the immediate vicinity.

Not for a moment did she doubt she and Saul were already stepping down the path of merging their lives together properly. Every minute she spent with him felt precious, fresh and new. If he had been anyone else the speed with which they had come together, joined together would have worried her. But he knew almost everything about her—and she him. This felt so natural, so right already it was impossible to imagine reverting back to mere friends.

Each grin, every exchange they had, cemented what she knew for fact now. She loved him. And he loved her.

Nothing else mattered.

As she finished turning another slow circle she jolted when she realised Saul had come to stand only a few paces behind her.

She smiled wryly at him.

"Still a bit jumpy, I suppose." She chuckled and moved slightly in the soft earth. "My tent faced this way, so when I climbed out of it I would have been about here."

Closing her eyes, she tried to mentally recreate that evening. Holding her hands out, she indicated the direction, then turned until the memory felt right again.

"I walked in this direction. Slowly. Carefully. Even with my shoes on I worried I'd trip and fall."

"No flashlight?" Saul interrupted in a low tone, curious but clearly not wanting to derail her train of thought.

Jennifer shook her head, tried to keep her eyes unfocused as she walked with measured steps, remembering every moment as best as she could.

"I had it in my pocket, just in case. When I'd listened outside my tent I could hear something. Scraping, a man's grunt now and then. I knew someone was out here and didn't want to attract undue attention."

A few times she paused, searching around the trees, seeking a similar setting to the one she recalled from that night. She'd been leaning against a large tree with flaky bark. She could bring forth the mental picture of the tableau, but there in the light of morning everything looked so similar, it was hard to judge.

"I couldn't have come too much further," she insisted, half to herself, half to Saul. "Time is different, of course, compared to being in the dark, the middle of the night. But it has to be around here somewhere."

Saul waited, patient and silent. Jennifer moved back and forth a bit, looking at different angles and checking for a tree that resonated with her memory. Many of the trees nearby her were too thin. She'd hugged hers, she remembered that, but her arms hadn't been able to close around the trunk.

As she moved, she spotted a group of trees that seemed to fit what she recalled.

"Maybe there." She pointed and hurried over.

Saul followed.

Jennifer moved from one to the next, frowning in deep thought. She swivelled her head left and right, trying to find which direction she would have seen the man.

"He was on a very faint downward slope," she finally said again. "It could have just been the dark and my imagination, but I think we should try over there."

She pointed to where her best guess was, hoping she wasn't leading them both on a wild goose chase. It also hadn't escaped her notice that despite his protests they hadn't been followed, Saul frequently surveyed their surroundings, his gaze clearly tracking for signs they'd been discovered or were being watched.

They'd gone on an incredibly round about, circular route in the car, doubling back, parking in shopping centres and stopping for petrol no less than three times while Saul bought snacks and drinks neither needed while he checked no one followed them. Paranoid hadn't even come close to the measures he'd taken to ensure their safety.

Jennifer couldn't believe anyone could possibly have traced them—her faith in Saul ran soul-deep. She felt safe with him, in his care.

They both bent over, searching the ground for signs of recently turned earth.

"Over here, maybe," Saul called out after a few minutes.

They'd split up, each taking different quadrants to cover the ground faster. Jennifer hurried over to where he knelt. The soil had clearly been recently overturned, but the area was smaller than she recalled. Frowning, she kept silent.

Saul removed a small hand trowel from his backpack and dug into the soft earth. Jennifer knelt beside him, her heart racing. The soil moved with ease, not having had time to compact. Within a few minutes Jennifer heard the dull thud as the blade hit what she assumed was the buried box. Saul dropped the tool and they both worked quickly with their hands to scrape away the last of the dirt, uncovering a prettily carved wooden box.

Wiping his hands on his jeans, Saul sat back and let her pick the box up.

Jennifer brushed the remaining earth from it, turning the object from side to side to admire the intricacies of the carvings. Vines wove around the outer edges, large ivy leaves and what looked like lotus flowers bloomed here and there. A delicate scene of a large lake with weeping willow, small birds in the sky and lilies covered the lid.

The box was beautiful, old and had been well maintained. Someone had loved this item, waxing it and keeping it pretty.

The thought he might return for it — perhaps soon — had her looking up and scanning their surroundings, nervous for the first time that day.

"I'm watching our backs," Saul said.

He rested his palm on her shoulder. The warmth of his touch comforted her.

"He can't have meant to leave this here for long," she replied. "This is gorgeous and has evidently been cherished for a number of years. Maybe we should go back to the car before we look inside?"

"Nah, it will only take us a minute. Besides, I don't want to take this back with us to London without knowing what it is. Depending on how dangerous it is we might want to leave it here, or rebury it somewhere else. I don't like working in the dark, I prefer to know what I'm involved in."

Jennifer nodded, seeing his point. She looked down at the box, ran the tips of her fingers over the gorgeous carvings, admiring it for a moment longer. Forgetting to breathe for the moment, anticipation rode her hard. Would there be jewels hidden within? Diamonds? Gold bullion? Every treasure-hunting daydream flittered through her mind.

Gathering her courage, she drew in a quick breath. Before she could change her mind, she cracked the lid open.

Disappointment deflated her mood instantly. Jennifer hadn't realised how ramrod straight her spine had been until crushing defeat had her slumping.

Papers, photographs and a few bundles of cash were neatly nestled inside the box.

"You were hoping for the crown jewels?" Saul commented, the fondness clear in his tone. "Weren't you? Gold? Gems maybe?"

"At the very least," she agreed. "Diamonds, winning Lotto tickets or long-lost gold bars or Spanish coins, maybe. What use are photos or maybe a couple thousand pounds of cash to me?"

Jennifer sat the box on the grass and picked up the neatly stacked piles of money and set them to the side.

Saul reached down and gathered a dozen or so pictures, studying them with a thoughtful look on his face.

Jennifer sifted through the remaining papers.

"Well here's something at least," she said.

Hidden down the bottom of the box underneath everything was a thin plastic key card—plain white with no markings except a barcode running along one edge—and a small USB memory stick.

"What do you think?" she asked.

Saul tore his gaze away from the photos and they exchanged glances. He took a brief look at the memory stick, then placed it carefully in the small coin pocket in his jeans.

Jennifer figured that other than her purse it was the safest place for it—better, in fact, since the chances of anyone taking the stick out of Saul's pocket was less than an attacker taking her purse.

While Saul scrutinised the key card, she turned her attention back to the photos. At first she flipped through the twelve or so prints, wanting to get an idea of what they were. Shots of stairwells, cement quads and a fire escape emergency exit had her scratching her head.

What the hell?

Two of the pictures had a woman partially in them. In one the tall, slender brunette had her back to the camera as she strode down a corridor towards what looked like a basement or storage room. With a knee-length, belted coat, long, loose curls falling down her back and knee-high boots it was almost impossible to say anything other than she was slender, Caucasian and had a wealth of warm brown hair.

In the other picture the frame was focused on an escalator going up a level. Long, plain white walls with embedded spotlights could have been inside any office building in the entirety of London. Indeed, Jennifer would have hazarded a guess that the people mover and building photographed could have been from anywhere in the whole world.

What made it noteworthy to her, however, was the dark-haired woman in what appeared to be the same coat stood amongst a group of people riding the escalator up to a higher floor. Her face was in profile and indistinct. Jennifer peered closely but could not make out anything that would help identify the woman.

"Do you think she's a target? Could this be a hit?" Jennifer's mind spun out of control as her imagination took over. "That would make the man I saw an assassin? Should we warn her?"

"Let's see what's on this memory stick first, babe," Saul replied.

Jennifer turned her head to look up at him. His grin was warm, indulgent. She had the strong suspicion he was trying hard to not laugh at her.

"These look like surveillance pictures to me," he continued. Flipping through them, he spread them out on the grass before her.

"See here, the wall of windows beside the escalator? That would be the perfect ambush place. A single shot—it wouldn't even have to be accurate or hit its intended target—would break all these planes. The sound of it would be phenomenal, like an avalanche of crashing glass, falling to these tiles. Also, it could be heard for miles around. Panic would ensue. People would run madly. A few more shots, just the mere sound of gunfire at this stage, would herd people wherever you wanted them—out onto the street or farther into the building, depending on the placement of who and where the bullets struck. Then here, this photo? This long corridor could easily be isolated. It's impossible to tell whether they need entrance to this area or whether they want to attack someone here, but look at these cameras here and here. See how they're a newer model than these here by the lifts? I bet that's important, possibly even the point of what our mystery man wanted to convey."

The clipped, rapid tone of Saul's voice mesmerised her. He sounded so professional, analysing the photos and spotting things she hadn't seen or had merely taken for granted. The way he'd described the various scenarios that could unfold so simply took her breath away.

It was a side of him she'd never seen.

Jennifer didn't know how she felt about that. Calmed that Saul could obviously predict what might occur, but also saddened that this doubtlessly came from experience. That he'd made such plans many times before, or had helped carry such missions out.

"...I don't recognise the building though. These pictures are all so generic. It might not even be here in London. I can think of many places worldwide that would fit this modern architecture. And without date stamps these pictures could be five, even ten years old."

"They mightn't be relevant to anything," Jennifer pointed out. "As you say, these pictures might be old, out of date or even unusable for whatever purpose the man had. If he needed them he wouldn't bury them, right?"

"But if there was no value to them, Vincent and his mate wouldn't have ambushed you at your flat, tried to kidnap or threaten you. No, there must be some purpose to them, something we're not seeing."

Saul's furrowed his brow, deep in thought.

Jennifer remained silent, looking over the photos again, focusing on the smaller details in the hopes of spotting something useful. Her instinct said the pictures were based in London, but she couldn't really spot anything conclusive to prove it so. There were no signs that she could see, so she couldn't swear the predominant language was English. Neither were there shops or anything useful to act as a reference point.

Indeed, the few people in the photos mostly wore overcoats, scarves, beanies and cool-weather outerwear, and so give or take a decade it was impossible to firmly state anything other than it appeared modern.

"Okay, we need to read this memory stick," Saul interrupted her thoughts as he collected the photos into a pile. "But I don't have the capabilities to learn anything about this key card. I want to call in a marker from a colleague, on the quiet, not officially. Are you okay with that?"

"Do you trust this person?"

"To a high degree yes." Saul shrugged when she looked at him, waiting for a fuller explanation. "I don't trust him as much as I trust you, or myself. But he's a mate, and more importantly he owes me a few favours. He's discreet and a good guy. Unless he feels we're doing something underhand or against the Agency, he'll keep quiet about helping us out."

"He's from the Agency?" Jennifer's interest piqued.

"One of our best analysts. The stuff he can do with encryptions and data mining is just unbelievable."

"I'd love to see where you work. But wait…if we're going in there why don't we ask Preston?"

"There's only so much I can ask of him without needing to bring it in officially," Saul explained. "Getting him to search out a name of a man who attacked you, that's one thing. If I brought this key card, the box, all if it to him, he'd need to officially ask one of the analysts, which would mean questions. No, this is better kept to ourselves for now, which means asking my mate personally and keeping it low key."

"Okay." Jennifer nodded, understanding his logic. "Let's see, it should take us around three hours to drive back, maybe less since it's Saturday. So let's guess we'll reach London around—"

"While I'll happily give you a tour, babe, people are there every day and at all sorts of odd hours. We're not your regular nine-to-five office, as I'm sure you know. I don't want to go into the office."

"Oh." Jenn frowned thoughtfully. "Well, what do we do, then?"

"We pray George is obsessed enough he owns almost all the equipment we need to read this key card and he's intrigued by our conundrum," Saul replied as he pulled out his mobile phone.

Jennifer packed the photos and bundles of cash neatly back into the box while Saul scrolled through his phone contacts. Selecting one, he then waited, turning the key card over in his free hand.

"George? Yeah, it's Saul. How's your weekend? Really? And after that, do you have plans this evening? I've got a bit of an issue that's cropped up, something off the books. I was hoping to call in a favour or two and get you to look at a memory stick and key card for me. It should be straightforward, but I don't want to mess it up or set off an internal encryption programme by mistake."

Saul wrinkled his nose, seemingly not pleased with his friend's response to his suggestion.

"Sure you owe me. Who got you those footy tickets when you were moaning about your father-in-law? Or the time I covered your arse and took the heat when you were streaming that video about the Russian twins? I'm serious here, man, don't yank my chain."

Jennifer lifted an eyebrow, a part of her deeply curious about the Russian twins' video. A deep, dark, secret spy agency, presumably waging war against the enemy to keep their country safe from harm, and one of the tech geeks was streaming porn?

Saul grinned at her, seeming to find her look amusing.

"Knew I could count on you. Look, we're three or so hours away. How about we swing by and pick up some curry, then you can help us out. Trust me, it should be a breeze. You'll have plenty of time to do your errands before your missus gets back from her shopping trip. Promise."

Saul stood, placed the key card in the pocket of his jeans then held out his hand to help Jennifer rise.

"Fantastic," Saul finished. "We'll see you then. Thanks, George."

Saul clicked his phone closed, then slid it into his shirt pocket. Jenn twined her fingers with Saul's. Holding the wooden box in her other hand, together they headed back to her campsite and his car.

"I thought you said he was a friend. It sounded to me like you had to twist George's arm," she said.

"Nah, he'll enjoy holding this over my head. I'll buy him a few beers next week. George loves it when field agents owe him. He lives for it."

"Do you really think the data will be encrypted?" she asked, recalling Saul's earlier comment on the phone that he didn't want to set anything off. "Wouldn't that indicate that the information was important? Or secret?"

"It's hard to say," Saul mulled. "So far we haven't really seen any indication that something's going on, let alone it's criminal. If it wasn't for those arseholes I'd be half tempted to say we're both blowing this out of proportion."

Jennifer remained silent as they made their way back to the car. She knew Saul believed her implicitly, that he knew something was going on, but they just couldn't work out what. A part of her hoped the memory stick and key card would answer some questions, or point them in the right direction.

She worried they'd run out of avenues to chase if they hit another dead end. Jennifer wasn't keen to act as bait, though if that was the only way to draw these men out into the open so they could discover what was happening, she might get desperate enough to do so. She refused to hide and cower, to alter her life because she'd seen a man burying this simple box.

"Hey," Saul said gently. He wrapped an arm around her and pulled her close to his body. "You're looking very serious there, babe. Are you all right?"

"Yeah, I'm hoping we get some answers. Nothing fits together and I'm starting to feel foolish."

"Don't," he insisted. "We're missing a large part of the bigger picture, that's why this isn't making sense. These seemingly small things are important enough— are so meaningful—that people out there we know nothing about are willing to hurt innocent strangers to acquire it. That points to something big. It will make sense once we get more details, I promise."

They drew up to the car. Saul gave her a squeeze, hugging her tightly. Jennifer wound her free arm around him, rising up on her toes to meet his lips with her own. They kissed and her world tilted once again.

Heat seared through her body, need crawled from her belly up her chest, her skin flushing hotly. She didn't register dropping the box onto the soft grass, only the desire to be as near as possible to Saul consumed her. Holding their bodies together, he pressed them closer, and moved his mouth hungrily over hers.

Lifting her hips, she enjoyed the thick hardness of his cock straining against his jeans. She moaned decadently, wishing they were both naked right now and she could guide him into her wet pussy.

Saul cupped her face, drawing away from her with reluctance.

"There is nothing I want more right now than to undress you slowly, worship every inch of your soft, delicious skin and make slow, exquisite love with you, babe." His tone conveyed the imminent 'but'. "Believe me, if we were in any other isolated forest, where we'd have a good chance of seclusion and privacy I wouldn't be talking, my tongue would be occupied in the far more pleasant task of tasting your sweet juices and making you scream my name. But considering how busy this place has been in the last week, and the fact I only have the one gun to protect us should we be attacked, I don't want to linger longer than necessary."

She groaned and pressed her face into his chest. Saul's clean scent felt like home to her. As she listened to the rapid pounding of his heart she could tell he was affected—that and the rock-hard shaft tenting his jeans, straining against his zipper, didn't need a diagram or explanation.

Lifting her head, she dropped a quick, practically chaste kiss to the edge of his chin, nipping him lightly with her teeth.

"You owe me," she purred, teasing him.

He flashed that wicked grin of his. "Absolutely."

Saul opened the passenger-side door for her. Thanking him, she climbed into the car, pleasantly occupied with fantasies of just how she could collect that marker later.

Chapter Six

"Do you have remote access to our databases?" Saul asked George over his shoulder.

Jennifer watched as George ran a hand through his scruffy brown hair. His dark-brown gaze was fixed upon the screen of his laptop as he scrolled through indecipherable — to her at least — code.

A moment passed. George didn't acknowledge Saul's words.

Jennifer grinned, amused. The man had looked sceptical when Saul had initially handed over the key card. George had turned it over in his hands and had peered at the barcode, reciting the numbers to himself in a soft tone. He'd then attached what appeared to be a swipe-card reader of some form by USB to his laptop. His fingers practically flew over the keyboard as weird squiggles and code flashed by, and promptly got lost in his own world from what Jennifer could ascertain.

"George!" Saul said loudly.

The man glanced up from his screen, blinking as if awakening from a dream.

"Sorry, mate, what was that?"

"Remote access to our database, how do I connect?"

"Oh, right." George leaned over, half standing out of his chair to type a few commands on the keyboard.

Jennifer and Saul both averted their gazes as George entered a long sequence into the password prompt and a new window popped open.

"Easy," George muttered, his attention returning fully to his own screen.

"Thanks," Saul replied, casting a laughing look to her.

Jennifer found herself liking George, his absolute attention to the task he did. Despite what she felt were his initial reservations, he now seemed completely engrossed in the card and whatever secrets it whispered to him. She wanted to ask what he was uncovering but figured interrupting him was stupid, and besides, he'd tell them sooner or later.

Meanwhile, she and Saul had found a few enormous JPEG and PDF files on the memory stick. When opened, they seemed to be scans of building blueprints. Even when they zoomed in close to the smaller notes, neither of them could find any distinct labels on the images.

"There's no descriptions," Jennifer said, pointing out the obvious. "So how are you going to search your work's databases to find out where these images refer to?"

Saul cast a pleased look at her.

"The dimensions are here," he replied. "We don't know where they are, but for the sake of ease I'll assume it's somewhere in central London—we can always expand the parameters if we come up blank. But if I search for buildings with rooms hosting these exact dimensions and specifications, hopefully we'll come across something. It will take time, but there can't be too many buildings with rooms exactly to these specifications."

Jennifer nodded. The plan seemed logical. Saul opened a bunch of tabbed windows and flipped between screens to enter in the details to various database search engines.

"What if these schematics are out of date? Or if they're blueprints for modifications that haven't been put onto any official database yet?"

"Now who's being paranoid?" Saul teased her. "Let's take one problem at a time. If this plan bombs we can think up something else, or rely on George to come up with something better."

Saul moved his fingers quickly over the keyboard as he entered search after search in consecutive windows. The clack of his keys made a strange symphony to Jennifer's ears, merging with the synonymous sound of George's typing. Once again she enjoyed this different side to her best friend. Having known him so long these small, never-before-seen aspects to his persona were like little gems.

She loved how her understanding and knowledge of this large, dark, powerful man grew more and more intimate the further they bared their souls to one another. Scooting her chair closer so she could watch the screen, Jennifer had to resist the urge to rest her head on Saul's shoulder.

"This might take a while," he warned her in a soft tone.

She smiled.

"I'm not going anywhere, it doesn't matter to me how long it takes."

Jennifer turned her face to press her lips into Saul's palm when he cupped her jaw. George was momentarily forgotten in the privacy of the special moment.

Saul moved his hand around to stroke the nape of her neck, caressing his fingers through her hair. The touch was not sexual, but her internal reaction, the heat that seared her, the desire that pounded in her blood belied the casual innocence of his fingers stroking her skin.

Need unfurled inside her stomach, her lust growing. Her clit throbbed. Wanting him to know the effect he had upon her senses, she nipped a teasing, biting kiss onto the soft pad of flesh at the base of his palm. He hissed, a sharp, hastily suppressed exclamation. Jennifer lifted her eyes to meet his gaze. Black eyes blazed hungrily at her. She grinned cheekily at him, pleased her message had been received.

Saul drew her face closer, bent his head and whispered naughtily in her ear, "If you're not careful, babe, you might bite off more than you can chew. I'm already hard as steel for you, the picture of your gorgeous blonde hair wrapped around my wrist as I fuck you hard from behind, plunging my cock balls-deep into your soaked pussy has been driving me mental since you ravished me out in the forest. I've been hard for so long I'm not in the mood for soft or gentle anymore, I want to take you hard, pound into you until you scream for me."

His words wove a spell around her, lust igniting through her body. Her nipples ached for his lips, her clit tingled with anticipation, and arousal had her pussy wet and willing for every dark, wicked promise he could dish out.

She raised her arm to wrap it around his neck, and was half out of her seat to straddle him and make him fulfil every word he'd uttered when she recalled

George not more than a few feet away from them. Stifling the groan, Jennifer instead gazed hotly at her lover.

Trying to get her sluggish brain to put together a coherent sentence even half as arousing as his words. The desktop pinged before she could utter a syllable. Saul didn't immediately move, holding her gaze and promising her all kinds of enticing adventures. Finally, lazily, he sat forward on his seat, a few keystrokes bringing up the hit from one of the architectural databases.

National Gallery — London.

Pictures, diagrams and information links were listed beneath the hit, offering a wealth of data connected with the find.

"The Gallery?" Saul said.

"Yeah," George said without looking up from his screen, his fingers still seeming to fly over the keys as code scrolled down. "Looks like your targets were thinking about a small heist. I still haven't narrowed down which exhibition they were interested in, but this security pass is fairly high level, they could have accessed most of the Gallery with it. More importantly, it's currently active — they could use it today, assuming, of course, it wasn't here with us."

"You knew it was the National Gallery?" Jennifer clarified, surprised.

"Oh, not until I started unlocking it," George assured her. "I'm just blown away by the details on this thing — their security firewalls suck. These guys are practically in the dark ages. A four year old with rudimentary hacking skills could crack this baby in a second. Really, it's almost a waste of my talent. Interesting though. They've got a list of all the pieces on show. It's been forever since I visited."

Jennifer couldn't believe how blasé George's attitude was. She glanced from him to Saul, back and forth again. George acted as if he saw this sort of thing every day and twice on Thursday...which in a sense she supposed he did. Still...

"Someone is going to break into the National Gallery." Jennifer cleared her throat, tried to get the slight croak out of her tone. "The London Gallery, and rob them. Uh, isn't this where we call the police? Or...panic? Do something?"

"We probably should bring this to Preston." George finally looked up from his screen to the two of them. "I don't think we can stop a heist ourselves, not considering the magnitude of effort that would have to go into such an enterprise."

Saul frowned, deep in thought. After a moment he spoke, "We still have no real details, though. It's all conjecture at this point. Sure, the security pass is still active, but we have it—not them. We have blueprints, diagrams and surveillance photos of ingress and egress points, but again, will it happen today? Next week? Did it occur three months ago and the Gallery merely covered it up? What, exactly, would we take to Preston? Supposition? Conjecture? He can't do anything about any of that."

"I agree with you," George said with a nod. "But this could blow up badly in your face if we sit on it. If we ignore this and something does happen...well, it won't matter we have nothing but smoke and mirrors. If management finds out we had forewarning, that we knew something was in the wind and we did nothing, our arses will fry."

"Well, we know what we think their target will be," Jennifer interjected. "And even though I was in school the last time I visited, the Gallery is bloody huge. Why don't we go there, have a look around. We can see if we recognise any of the areas from the surveillance photos. That at least would be another connection and something we can take to your Agency."

"I'm not sure I want you there," Saul replied. He roamed his gaze over her face possessively. "These people will know what you look like, and other than their names, we don't know anything about Vincent and his mate. It would be dangerous for you."

"At the National Gallery, with thousands of other visitors and tourists?" Jennifer replied. She took Saul's hand in hers, squeezing it gently. "Saul, we'll be careful, and surrounded by great big crowds of people. Look, you can call Preston and ask him if there's an update on Vincent if it will make you feel better. But honestly, what could possibly happen to me in such a huge place and with you right by my side?"

George shouted with a crack of laughter.

"Oh dear, you must be very new to all this. Those are words you never, ever say on a mission. Trust me."

Jennifer grinned, the mood having lifted with George's amusement. Saul, however, still looked torn. Jennifer pressed a kiss to his jaw.

"I'll be fine. I'll follow whatever orders you issue. I don't like the thought of you going there alone, and besides, this is my adventure too. I want to come along. Please."

Saul sighed.

"You better remember that tomorrow—your promise to follow my orders," he reiterated.

She smiled, glad he'd capitulated.

Saul saved copies of the blueprints and other maps of the National Gallery, emailing them to himself. Minutes later he started closing down the browsers.

"I owe you, George. Thanks, man," Saul said.

George nodded as he disconnected the card reader and ejected the plastic security pass. He looked at it a moment, then held it out to Saul.

"You realise we'll have to hand this in when we go to Preston, don't you?"

Saul nodded.

"Yeah. But I'd rather have it on me tomorrow when we check out the Gallery. I doubt we'll need it, but I'll feel better having it in my pocket. Can you sit on this for a day?"

"Sure," George said. "It'll be Sunday, anyway. No one from management will be in, and even if we talked to Preston I doubt he'd call them in with what we have. One day won't make a difference."

The two men stood and shook hands. Jennifer grinned as George turned to her and she returned his handshake.

"It was lovely to meet you," she said with feeling.

He chuckled.

"You too. I presume I'll be seeing you around?"

"Jennifer will be around," Saul replied as he wrapped an arm possessively across her shoulders.

She grinned happily up at him. "Maybe for a beer or dinner one night down at the local pub?"

"Sounds good. I'll see you Monday, man."

George walked them out.

When they'd climbed into the car, Saul revved the engine, peeled away from the kerb. Jennifer looked around them, half expecting to see someone trying to follow them. When it became clear no one was behind the car, she turned to look curiously at Saul.

"I wasn't kidding back there," he said without taking his attention from the road. "I'm burning up for you, babe. We could teleport back to my place and it still wouldn't be quick enough for my liking."

Jennifer sat back in her seat, her desire instantly flaming once again. She nodded. More promising words weren't necessary when she felt exactly the same. He knew it and she knew it.

"Step on it," she ordered.

* * * *

They started kissing before Saul had even closed the door behind them.

Ravenous for him, Jennifer clasped his shoulders with her hands, scraping her blunt nails over his skin as she tried to remove his shirt and jacket. His buttons popped and she didn't feel the least bad. His clothes were the enemy, hiding the beauty of his body from her.

Saul tugged her shirt up over her head, exposing her lacy bra to the cool air. He pressed his body against hers. She shivered as her naked back hit the chilly wall. They each grappled with shoes, waistbands and finally each other's underwear.

"I need to feel you," she panted, devouring the sight of his luscious, muscled body with her gaze.

Saul didn't reply—a small grunting sound of assent emanated from his lips instead.

His hands were warm on her bare hips. He swung her around from the wall, pivoting so she faced the back of the couch.

"Hold onto it," he said.

She clasped her hands onto the top of the backrest, looking over her shoulder at him. He'd ducked for a moment, digging one hand into his crumpled jeans for a foil packet. As he sheathed his thick cock Jennifer's mouth watered.

She'd wanted to suck him, feel his head spurt and tremble beneath her tongue. They were both too worked up for a long, slow mouth-fuck, though, the intricate, intimate dance of back-and-forth between them having burnt and built for too long throughout the day. Saul tugged her hips back, causing her to bend over — her naked arse waggling in the air.

"Damn, I want to fuck that arse," Saul ground out hotly.

Cream pooled slickly in her pussy. How could such simple words make her so aroused? Particularly when she'd never performed that specific act and until discovering the magic between them, hadn't felt the least desire to do so.

Saul reached one hand around from her pelvis, spreading her arse cheeks until he could stroke a finger over the tiny, puckered opening of her anus. His digit seemed to find a whole host of nerve endings, each one jolting to life and telling Jennifer in no uncertain terms why some women enjoyed that decadent act so much.

"Shit," she panted, all other words flying out of her mind. She arched her back, pushing her arse farther into his reach.

"I don't have the patience for that tonight," he said sadly, "but I do think we'll go there some other time. For now, though..."

After a few more strokes he lowered his hand to slide nimbly over her soaking lips and eagerly sought out the heat of her clit. Her eyes fluttered shut as he rubbed over her nub with devastating skill.

She moaned loudly and wriggled her arse into him, begging silently for more.

"That's my girl," he crooned. "Do you know how gorgeous you look? Naked as sin, bum in the air as I prepare you for my cock?"

She felt three long, thick fingers enter her swiftly, pumping and stretching her channel. She groaned, unable to find words to reply.

"Oh yeah, take all of me, that's it."

Rocking back, eagerly accepting his penetration, Jennifer craved more. After a whole day of their mutual teasing and swift, too-brief touches and stolen, hot kisses she was horny as hell. She needed him as hard and fast as he'd promised her so darkly earlier.

"Fuck me," she pleaded, pushing her hips to entice him. "Hard. Fast. Right now, like you said."

"Holy shit," Saul cursed, the strain in his voice showing his control was as thin as hers.

He removed his fingers from her clenching pussy, lifted his hand around to press down at the base of her spine, tilting her arse farther up. In one long, slow stroke he moved inside her, his cock piercing her with an intensity that stole her breath.

Deeper and deeper he thrust, the motion continuing forever. His inches seemed endless, until finally he stopped, his balls slapping lightly against her.

"Hang on, babe," he murmured huskily.

Saul grabbed hold of her hips and pulled out of her only to slam back in again. At the different angle she stood at, his shaft pressed over a different set of nerves, including her G-spot. The stimulation was intense, but still she craved more. Jennifer released one hand from the back of the couch to caress her clit. That, coupled with Saul removing his cock and again possessing her quickly ratcheted up her excitement.

Harder and faster they both came together, the only sound in the room was their gasping, panting breaths. Jennifer groaned, her climax building somewhere between her belly and pussy. Her skin prickled with sensation, the thick possession of Saul's cock driving her wild.

He slammed into her, over and over, stealing her breath in the same way that he'd taken her heart. All too soon the pleasure burst and she felt as if she exploded into tiny pieces.

Screaming her orgasm, she shouted Saul's name, the pleasure more than intense — it bordered on painful.

"Fuck yes, just like that, babe," he cried out, his thrusts deeper and harder. Suddenly, he shuddered and pumped his seed deeply within her body. Saul dug his hands into her hips, holding her still as he emptied himself.

They stood frozen like that for a moment, locked together.

Finally, her legs shook with reaction as the adrenaline faded.

Saul carefully pulled his cock out of her, scooped one arm under her legs and swept her up close to his body.

Feeling sated and blissful, Jennifer wrapped an arm around his neck and pressed her forehead to his chest.

"I needed that," she murmured.

He carried her to the bedroom and gently placed her on the mattress. She tilted her head up and they shared a lingering, tender kiss.

"I'll be right back," he whispered.

She watched while he removed the latex, and left the room. After a moment she heard the tap water running.

Shaky, but with her skin still highly sensitised, Jennifer pulled the blankets down and crawled between the sheets. Lying on one side she waited for Saul to rejoin her. He didn't take long. As comfortable as if they'd been together for years, he climbed next to her in the bed, entwining their arms together with familiar ease.

"I can't imagine this getting any better," he confessed.

She smiled.

"I can. The more we learn about each other and the closer we get, the more special this will become. Just think of all those tiny, intimate details we have to learn about one another. I can't wait to learn them all, and see all these other sides to you I never knew about before. I get a thrill of excitement just thinking about it."

"Well, when you put it like that." He chuckled. Saul bent to lick and nibble a slow trail down the side of her neck.

Jennifer shivered in delight—she had quite a few erogenous nerves at the base of her neck in the juncture of her collarbone.

"Mmm," Saul murmured. "I see what you mean. I can't wait to explore every inch of you."

She laughed huskily, more than willing to start right there and then.

Chapter Seven

It had been more than a decade since Jennifer had stood inside the National Gallery, but the magnificence of the architecture still had her gaping in amazement. High-soaring ceilings, the dome, intricately carved cornices—the whole place was stunning.

She and Saul had spent almost two hours roaming around, appearing as nothing more than innocent locals whiling away a late Sunday morning. Hand in hand, their fingers entwined, they looked...well, exactly like the lovers they were. Surely no one could mistake the glances they shot at each other, or the possessive way Saul leaned close when he pointed something out to her—or she to him.

"There are only three exhibits the Gallery is promoting, but there's so much more here. They could be after anything," Jennifer commented, feeling slightly overwhelmed. Some of her jitters had returned too. Preston had reported he had suspicions Vincent and a man who fitted the description of this associate, Graeme, hadn't been seen since mid-afternoon the day before.

Despite the safety she felt with Saul, her nerves were unsettled, her instincts knowing those men were both loose somewhere, possibly lurking under the radar.

"I've seen some very strange things over the years," Saul replied. He squeezed her hand and her heart fluttered, focusing her attention on him again. "If it's a private collector instigating this then he could literally be after anything. It might be an obscure sculpture no one has heard of, or one of these beginners might be his estranged son and have massive sentimental attachments and no inherent monetary value at all. It's impossible to say."

Jennifer nodded and stared at the painting they stood before.

The local art school had been given a tiny corridor, which they'd dedicated to their internal award winners. Amateurs, but already incredibly talented, the running theme seemed to be the individual's own personal take on more famous work. A statue clearly mimicking the famous Venus was of a bustier, larger woman with short, cropped hair. The Mona Lisa had been transferred into a well-known politician, the secretive smile seeming far more sinister now than the famous painting.

All sorts of well-recognised Masters had clearly influenced the winners.

But Jennifer had been ensnared by a beautiful beach landscape. A tall, dapper black man in a navy blue, thinly pinstriped suit danced with a svelte, Caucasian blonde woman in a slinky, glittery cocktail dress. It took her a moment to place the original — The Singing Butler.

Realising she'd been staring at the painting, Jennifer glanced at Saul. His gaze roamed the vivid colours and bold strokes also. She smiled fondly at him, pleased to see him as enthralled by the romantic image as she.

"It's captivating," he said. "I like the way his arms cradle his love. There's an inherent gentleness in the way he's guiding her."

"They seem to be leading each other," she postulated. "Facing each other while they dance, but with their torsos angled so their backs are turned to us they're equals. Because they're moving away from the viewer and captured in that moment you can't see who's in control. How can you tell he's guiding her? She might be in the lead."

Saul chuckled.

"Is a woman ever really not in charge of her man?"

Jennifer grinned but was clever enough not to answer that.

"I wonder if the tide's coming in or going out?" she mused. Jennifer had meant to merely think the query, but such personal thoughts had a habit of slipping out when she was with Saul. Her guard was always relaxed around him, she trusted him implicitly. No thought was too strange or too personal to share with him.

"They're just enjoying the moment," Saul said. "It doesn't matter how much longer they have, or whether the sea is turning towards them or not. They're dancing now, lost in each other and clearly deeply in love with one another. That's what they're holding onto."

"The more I look at it, the more I love it," she replied with a soft smile. She enjoyed the bold, bright colours, the confident, sure strokes left from the brush, but most of all she loved the promise and fantasy the painting represented for her. Jennifer could so clearly imagine herself and Saul on such a warm, isolated beach, dressed to the nines, dancing together, lost in each other. It could represent them today, next week, six months into the future and hopefully when they were both old and grey, fifty years from now.

"I think I'll get this," Jennifer said.

At exactly the same time Saul commented, "I think I'll ask how much this is."

They glanced at each other. Jennifer laughed.

Saul cupped her jaw, bent down and pressed his lips to hers. They shared a slow, searching kiss. Her eyes fluttered shut and she drank in the intimacy of the moment.

"It can be the first purchase we make together," Saul finally said when he pulled back.

Her brain scrambled, it took a second for Jennifer to recall what they were talking about.

"The painting, yes," she murmured. "I think buying it together, for both of us, would be perfect."

Jennifer rested her head against Saul's shoulder and they stared at the painting for another minute, each lost in their own thoughts. Jennifer daydreamed about what a life together for the two of them would entail. In some ways it would be no different. They'd been friends for so long, catching up over dinner or seeing a movie with each other was practically routine. In other ways she'd learnt so much about Saul over this weekend he was a whole new man to her.

Intriguing. Dangerous. Exciting. Reliable.

She couldn't wait to learn more about him, grow with him.

Saul made a slight turn, asking wordlessly if she was ready to go. She moved with him and they made their way back. En route Saul constantly turned his head as he glanced around. At first she assumed he was staring at all the amazing artwork that filled every nook, but then she understood that wasn't it at all.

"The security here is impressive," he said in a hushed voice so they wouldn't be overheard in the near-silent halls. "There are well-trained guards at most of the exhibit entrances, motion detectors, and I'm sure those red lights indicate some of the most up-to-date heat and infrared sensors. The security company logo is the same group we use for training, Firthington. They're one of the best, cutting edge, not just here in London, but on a global scale."

Jennifer tried to keep up with Saul's commentary. "If there's so much security, and multiple layers by the sound of it, too, not just simple alarms, then is it realistic to believe the place might be burgled? I mean, we're not in a movie here. All these systems set in place would have to be neutralised, probably simultaneously. That's not for some eccentric, rich father who has lost touch with his artistically talented son. This sounds professional and scary."

"It would certainly need a team, a well-rehearsed, savvy group of individuals who already have trust in each other. That's not as common as you'd think. Usually such talented people work alone, or at most in pairs. If you don't trust the people you're doing a mission like this with…well, let's say usually you're not a long-term problem."

They were near the main entrance hall now. They walked up to one a large desk area where a number of men and women in well-cut suits talked in hushed voices to other browsers. Almost immediately one of the men caught Saul's gaze. He said a quick last word to the women then ambled over to them. His brass name plate had 'Nick' engraved into it.

"I'd like to enquire about the cost of one of your paintings, The Dancers, by Lazray Haughton," Saul said in a smooth tone.

The man smiled in what seemed a well-practiced motion and nodded. "Of course, sir. If you'll let me go bring that piece up on our files we can discuss terms and..."

Jennifer tuned Nick out as they moved to a different section and he logged onto a thin, wireless laptop.

"...and it's the first piece Mr Haughton has exhibited. I'm sure he'll be thrilled to know a lovely couple such as yourselves are interested in it. Now, it says here in his record that he's amenable to selling the canvas, and the Gallery offers a wonderful deal on service and crating with delivery if you'd just care to..."

Listening with half an ear, Jennifer almost missed it when Saul did a visible double take. Following his gaze, she saw he watched a man and a woman as they crossed the enormous foyer. Jennifer couldn't spot anything unusual about them and wondered why they had grabbed Saul's attention.

The man was very tall, six foot three or four at least. His dark hair was lightly salted with grey and neatly trimmed. His build was that of an ex-athlete—toned and he was evidently fit, but no longer at his peak. In jeans and a shirt he looked in no way remarkable from any of the dozens of other men whom she'd seen today.

The woman barely came to his shoulders, though Jennifer noticed she wore comfortable sneakers and not high heels. She was fit in the manner of a gymnast—all lean muscle. But it was the wealth of straight, auburn-red hair that set her apart from other women. Dressed similarly to her partner in jeans and a simple, prettily patterned shirt, Jennifer couldn't deduce from watching them why Saul's gaze lingered on them for almost a minute.

They both looked so normal.

Deeply curious now, she tilted her head back to Saul.

"Do you know them?" she asked.

He gave her a short nod. Meeting her eyes, he held them, seeming to try to will her to understand something. "Yes. From work."

Surprised, she widened her eyes and snapped her head back to stare again at the couple. They were completely un-noteworthy.

Though...the more she watched them...Jennifer realised they both scanned the cavernous room. Yet neither of them appeared to notice the artwork on display, let alone admire it. They both watched the people around them. The manner in which the man, in particular, held himself reminded her somehow of Saul.

Perhaps it was because they had similar training, or maybe just the knowledgeable, defensive outlook both men would need in their professions – something screamed about his posture that he was completely aware of his surroundings and ready at a moment's notice to spring into action.

The woman, his partner, was no slouch either. Jenn could see her moved her head around as they roamed the room. The action reminded Jennifer of a laser beam, taking in everything, calculating and analysing. The way she held herself, her free hand loosely hanging by her side, palm cupped towards her body, reminded Jennifer of an old gunslinger, waiting for the indication to snatch for their weapon, crouch and fire.

"We haven't said anything to...your boss. Why would there be co-workers of yours here?" Jennifer asked.

Saul shook his head, clearly not wanting to answer further.

Her attention reverted to Nick, who still smiled amiably but now appeared both puzzled and worried he might have lost his sale. Jennifer smiled as charmingly as she could at him.

"I'm sorry, Nick," she said, her attention fully on the man now. "You were saying that deliveries only occur on weekdays? Would it be possible for the item to be delivered early in the evening? That would suit us best."

"Of course," Nick replied with relief. "Now I'll just need a few details from you both."

Jennifer stole a glance over her shoulder. She saw the backs of the other agents as they left the main room and headed into one of the exhibits. Wondering if they should split up and she should follow, she exchanged a glance with Saul. He shrugged a shoulder then took her hand in his and gave it a squeeze, but didn't let go. That answered that question, they'd not be splitting up. Saul gave Nick the information he required, though his mind was clearly elsewhere.

Keeping part of her attention on Saul and Nick, Jennifer scanned the busy room, bursting with curiosity about the other agents. Her mind filled with questions. Was the Agency already aware of something being planned here? Was the Agency part of it? She frowned at this. Surely Saul would be have known if that was the case? But then...he couldn't possibly know every mission going on, that wouldn't be logical.

Her mind worked, trying to fit the pieces of the puzzle together. She'd unconsciously tuned out both her lover and the museum employee as she grew lost in her own musings, her gaze wandering over the other patrons.

It took her a moment to realise her attention had been captured by a striking woman who walked quickly across the room. Her heels clacked on the tiles, her long, brown curls bouncing down her back as she moved smoothly towards her destination.

She wore a subtle, navy blue blazer with pencil-slim skirt and a photo identity card identical to the other Gallery employees. Focused on her smartphone, she clearly knew exactly where she was headed, for she didn't glance up from the small screen.

Recognition crashed over Jennifer, like being hit by a wave.

"Saul," she said with a tug to her lover's arm. Tilting her chin, she indicated the woman.

It was the lady in the photos they'd uncovered in the wooden box. Saul must have understood exactly who she was, too, for his whole body froze.

Still texting on her phone, the woman appeared oblivious to their attention. Jennifer followed the direct line she walked in with her gaze and realised she headed for a door along one of the walls, marked clearly as 'Employees Only, Unauthorised Personnel Not Admitted'.

"Oh, Saul," Jennifer murmured. "She's going into that door. We'll lose her."

Without waiting for him to say anything, Jennifer pulled away and moved hurriedly towards the woman.

"Wait! Jenn, you can't just—damn it."

She heard him shout behind her. Jennifer didn't pay attention. She focused on catching up to the brunette. The sound of Jennifer's heeled boots rushing closer finally appeared to capture the woman's attention. She looked up from her phone.

Jennifer drew up to her, huffing a little. A blush stole over Jennifer's face as she realised she had no clue what to say to the lady without sounding like an imbecile. She glanced at the woman's security pass, noticing her name stencilled in block letters beneath the obligatory awful face shot.

Chelsea Atchison.

"Uh," Jennifer started. "Hi, Chelsea. I'm Jennifer Mabbot, and this is going to sound very strange, but do you know...um... That is, have you been approached by any strange men here lately? I mean..."

Blushing harder, Jennifer struggled for words, not even knowing where to start. The woman appeared puzzled but polite enough. Jennifer didn't need to turn when she felt Saul come up behind her. Chelsea's eyes widened slightly and she studied Saul intently.

Frowning, Jennifer cast a quick glance at Saul, seeing he scrutinised the brunette as well.

What the hell?

A closer look, however, showed her that Saul appeared to be focusing on remembering something. He wasn't merely having a stare at the pretty woman. Her feminine instincts settled with that understanding, and Jennifer wondered what it was she seemed to be missing.

An almighty crack rent the air. It sounded like the world around her imploded. Jennifer turned instinctively to look. The huge floor-to-ceiling windows shattered and fell as if in slow motion. Peering out amongst the entrance driveway and through the columns, Jennifer couldn't see what had caused the windows to break.

A loud *whoosh* sounded before one of the many pillars exploded.

There was a moment of shocked silence, then the air filled with screams as people ran in every direction.

Saul knelt to the ground, pulling Jennifer down beside him.

Chelsea, rather than screaming hysterically as a good portion of the other women at present were, crouched into a classic defensive posture. She drew a large handgun out of her bag and turned her head to scan the area in what Jennifer was coming to understand as a highly professional surveillance of the room.

"You're a part of this?" Saul ground out at Chelsea, pushing Jennifer behind him as he used his body to shield her.

Chelsea cast him a quick, disinterested glance before returning her attention to her surroundings. "Not now," she snapped. "I can't quite place you, but I'm certain I've seen you before. Dublin?"

"No, I'm London based. Who the fuck are you?"

The room was over half empty now, the patrons stampeding towards every door in a mad scramble to escape. One series of steps, however, appeared to be getting louder, not retreating.

Jennifer looked around and spotted a slender man in a large overcoat hurrying towards them. He was speaking, but no one was around him. His hand cupped the side of his face. His hair fell forward like a wave, partially concealing him. He reached with his fingers to tuck the strands behind his ear in a gesture

Jennifer recognised. Saul had stood, dragging Jennifer with him, when he'd noticed the approach of the other man.

"That's him!" she blurted out, caught somewhere between fear and excitement. "Saul, that's the man from the forest, I'm almost positive."

He drew his own gun and started moving them both backwards, Jennifer still protected behind his body.

"I just knew you'd be trouble the moment I realised you'd seen me bury that damn box," the man complained as he came to stand beside Chelsea. Turning to face Chelsea, he spoke his next words directly to her. "Someone's got an itchy trigger finger. This whole thing has gone to hell. I say we leave before our positions are compromised."

"What about McIlroy? What does he think?" Chelsea replied in a hurried tone.

Saul stiffened again, his head turning from one to the other of them.

Jennifer was completely at a loss. She trusted Saul, though, without a single doubt. If he felt they were in danger he'd get them out. Since he hesitated, she knew something else was happening beneath the surface.

"McIlroy?" Saul interrupted. "You're from the Dublin branch?"

Both the man and Chelsea stared at him. Recognition lit in her eyes and her stance relaxed infinitesimally.

"Of course, I've seen you in the group meetings. Preston Jones is your boss, right?"

"He's Agency?" the man verified.

Chelsea nodded.

He seemed to make a snap decision. "David Greer, and you've met Chelsea Atchison. We're under deep cover right now, have been for almost eighteen months. We're on loan, you could say."

"Okay, well that fills in a few blanks, but I still think —" Saul started but David cut him off.

"The rest of the team are only minutes away, and they aren't Agency, even though we're currently with them. We need to split up and leave, right now. McIlroy has dealt with Vincent and Graeme. They've been taken in and are being held as hostile witnesses. They're a part of our case. We'll file a report later, we have to go."

"They were supposed to tell you phase two was being instigated before the attack happened," Chelsea insisted to David.

He shrugged and took a gentle hold of her arm. "We need to move, Chelsea. Right now. I suggest you both leave with all the other innocents," he said to Saul.

"But —" Jennifer had a dozen questions on the tip of her tongue, most important of all whether David was sure he had the right men in custody. She wanted to know what the hell he meant by 'holding them as hostile witnesses' and what that would entail. But Saul had taken hold of her hand and headed in the direction of one of the emergency exits. David and Chelsea were moving deeper inside the Gallery.

"Saul, hang on. They haven't explained...well much of anything!" she insisted.

He cast her a glance over his shoulder but kept walking at a fast pace. She recognised the grim determination on his face and sighed, going along with him for now, but swearing she'd get some answers very, very soon.

They evacuated the building.

Chapter Eight

"They're Agency," Saul said once they were in view of the street. The simple way he made the statement showed that to him it really was that easy. "If Preston doesn't know right now what's going on, twenty minutes after I call and update him he sure as hell will discover what's happening."

Jennifer had to walk fast to keep up with Saul. When he noticed, he shortened his strides but kept up a quick pace.

"If David, or his branch have Vincent and Graeme in custody, how could Preston not know? And how can they hold onto them when surely it should be me who presses charges against him?"

"I'm more disappointed I couldn't come face to face with those arseholes first," Saul replied grimly. "I had a few choice...words...I meant to get across to them."

Jennifer huffed out a nervous laugh. She rushed to come up side by side with Saul and took his hand in hers. She squeezed his fingers gently and decided it might be best to change the subject.

"Didn't Chelsea say she'd seen you in a meeting?"

"Those monthly meetings have upwards of two hundred people at them, remotely and in various offices," Saul explained. "Though I am curious how their mission wasn't mentioned in any of the minutes. A catalogue of all on-book and in-progress activities is supposed to be submitted."

"Sounds like they're not official," Jennifer mused.

Saul nodded as they approached his car. She was well used to his instinctive courtliness, opening the doors for her. Oddly, though, he rested a hand against the window of the car and carefully studied each direction around them. Since he did this silently, she didn't interrupt.

Even more bizarrely, Saul crouched to the wet pavement, tilting his head almost to the ground. He looked under the car, scanning the undercarriage carefully. Part of her brain insisted the chances that there would be a bomb or something similar planted on the car was insane. But then, she similarly would have assumed not half an hour ago the chances of gunfire at the National Gallery, the giant windows being smashed and the alarms sounding, was also utterly impossible.

She remained silent as Saul checked the car thoroughly.

Seeming satisfied, he stood up and wrapped his hands around her shoulders, pressing her back against the outside of the vehicle.

"I was so worried for you," he stated, his tone deadly serious.

Jennifer threaded her arms about his waist, drawing his body close to hers. Saul leant down and kissed her tenderly. They moved their lips slowly, delicate and almost reverent in their desire.

Her heart soared. This was so easy, this burgeoning, new relationship between them. Better than that, it felt so right, so good. Jennifer couldn't imagine her life any other way, not ever.

She clung to him, waves of pleasure shooting through her body as she lifted her hips to rub herself into his delicious muscles. Saul lifted his hands, held her jaw and tilted her head. At the new angle, he could penetrate her mouth deeper, plunder her with his tongue.

Moaning, Jennifer arched her back.

"Oh, no," she whispered when he finally pulled back. Instantly she wanted to taste Saul again, feel his mouth roam over hers, explore him lower. Forgetting for the moment they stood in the middle of central London, Jennifer wanted nothing so much as to find somewhere warm and comfortable, strip them both naked and lick every delectable part of his dark, luscious body.

Slowly.

Inch by inch.

Something of her thoughts must have reflected in her eyes, for Saul grinned wickedly at her.

"You're going to get me into a world of trouble," he rumbled. He unlocked her door and held it open for her as he continued, "I can just see myself trying to talk our way out of a public exposure and performance of indecent acts charge. 'But you see, Officer, my woman is so hot I couldn't resist. She gets this look in her eye and unconsciously licks her lips and my cock stiffens and I can't help myself.'"

Jennifer laughed. She reached out to caress his cheek as she moved past him, then slid into the passenger seat. He climbed in next to her, sitting behind the wheel, then dug his phone out, pressed a few buttons and held it to his ear.

"David Greer and Chelsea Atchison," Saul said sharply. "Dublin branch. Jenn and I just bumped into them at the National Gallery. Apparently they're working undercover and the Gallery's in a shambles. They have Vincent and Graeme in custody—some man called McIlroy over there is in charge."

"Son of a bitch." She could hear Preston's curse from next to Saul. Curious, Jenn leaned closer in to hear both sides of the conversation. "No wonder we couldn't find either of them and there'd been no activity in any of their accounts. Let me make some calls, crack some balls. But McIlroy is a good person. If his team says those two are locked down, they're not going anywhere. Give me a bit of time to make some calls. The two of you should come down here. I've a mountain of paperwork for you to get started on."

"Great," Saul sighed. "We'll be down there soon, but only for an hour or two."

"Fine."

Saul disconnected the call and placed the phone on the dashboard. Jenn caught his gaze as he slowed for an intersection. He seemed tired but resigned. She took his hand and squeezed it.

"It'll be good to get some answers," she said.

He nodded. "Hopefully. It sounds like there might be some internal politicking going on. But Preston will get what we need, I'm sure."

* * * *

"I'm still trying to get all the details," Preston said the moment Saul walked into his office. "McIlroy is strangely difficult to reach just now. But I've spoken to a few others over there in Dublin. Vincent and Graeme are locked down tight and will remain so. I've threatened to tear holes into everyone down there if either smells fresh air before they're thrown into a cage and scheduled for court. You can tell Jennifer she's safe."

"Nice to see I wasn't the only one in the dark here," Saul replied mildly. Beneath his calm exterior he was still angry as hell at the entire situation, though not at his boss personally. He'd left Jennifer at his desk, clearly interested in his work area and making friends with a few of his colleagues.

"I've managed to confirm Atchison and Greer are indeed ours, from Dublin," Preston said as he laced his fingers behind his head. "No one there has any inkling if they have changed sides—or if they do, they aren't sharing that information. Right now I'm not sure they'd even tell us whether they thought their Agents were turned or not. I've put pressure on some of their team leaders—pointing out an innocent bystander was not only drawn into the mission unwillingly, but also nearly harmed. They didn't appear to be paying attention until I brought you into the equation and threatened to potentially take over. That's when they started making noises."

"I'm not going to get to see either Vincent or Graeme, am I?" Saul scowled.

"I know where you're coming from," Preston shook his head. "And believe me, if Felicity had been in the same circumstance I'd likely be just as eager as you are now to get a message through to these men. But right now I would prefer you lay low, with Jennifer. Find a cosy, secluded B&B and hole up there for a week."

"You've already got someone looking into this?" Saul replied, surprised.

"No. Actually I was intrigued when you mentioned you saw Rob and Eleanor at the Gallery. Not being a man who easily believes in coincidence, I tapped a mate of mine in their division. He was cagey, would only say that they were on what he believed was an unrelated mission and that he'd get back to me once he'd checked it out for himself."

"Do you think they were investigating David and Chelsea?"

"It's impossible to say, but if the Fire and Ice team are looking into our colleagues from Dublin I'd be tempted to back right the hell off and go somewhere nice for a week on the work budget."

Saul thought about what Preston had told him.

Rob and El were known throughout the Agency as the 'problem solver' team. Frequently referred to as Fire and Ice — whether it was in reference to the term Shock and Awe, or El's red hair and Rob's frequently icy demeanour, Saul didn't know.

Suddenly, though, a week at the seaside with Jenn appealed far more. This case already had too many agents hovering around it.

"I'd like to at least be appraised of what's happening in it," Saul finally said.

They both knew he was on the edge of capitulating and merely stating his terms.

Preston nodded. "When I know, you will."

Saul agreed and stood. They shook hands.

"Where are you guys headed?" Preston asked, sounding genuinely curious.

"The Isle of Wight," Saul replied. "We've been down there a number of times in groups with friends. I know Jenn is particularly fond of a few places down that way. I'll bring my laptop, stay in touch. It'll be good to get away for a while, though, especially considering the hectic weekend we've had."

Preston grinned. "I'm sure you'll both manage quite comfortably."

Saul left Preston's office. After scanning the large area, he found Jenn with George at his desk. The two of them had their heads bent over George's computer screen, peering at something. Saul came up behind them and laid a hand on Jenn's shoulder. She cast a fleeting glance up at him accompanied by a ravishing smile that nearly caused his heart to stop.

"George has all these cool cheating codes for computer games," she said as she turned back to the screen. "Look at this one, I can have unlimited — "

"I'm hoping when I get you down to the beach you'll find better ways to pass the time," Saul commented, feeling smug at the surprise he had for her.

Instantly Jenn's full attention swung in his direction. A very primitive, egotistically masculine part of him loved how she focused completely on him, as if nothing and no one else in the world were present.

"The beach?" she repeated. "We're going down to the Isle of Wight? Oh, have you booked that little place down the road from the old ice cream parlour? I love it there, though it's not really paddling weather."

"We can walk down the beach wrapped up in our winter gear," Saul insisted.

Jenn laughed. Oh shit, how he loved that laugh of hers. He wished she'd use it more often. He made a personal vow to surprise her often, give her small things just to hear that husky laughter full of sin and sex.

"I need to make a couple of calls when we get back to my place, but yeah, that's the plan. For a whole week."

Saul's breath hitched as Jenn gazed at him with those searing, beautiful eyes of hers. He always felt stripped bare beneath her, as if she could see into the most secret core of his heart. He loved her more than words could ever come close to expressing.

"Did you get answers?" she asked.

Saul shrugged, knowing he couldn't discuss much in front of George just yet. Despite the fact he trusted his mate, the mission—what little he knew of it, anyway—was being strictly compartmentalised.

"Some. It got us a paid week at your favourite place. You're safe, though—the bastards are under lock and key. They're not going anywhere."

"Nice for some," George grumbled good-naturedly. "Meanwhile I get called in—on my night off, no less—to sift through boatloads of data. Some dipshits shot up the Gallery and now I have to—oh. Oh...really?"

Saul took Jenn's hand in his when she snickered, unable to contain her laughter. George looked from her to him and his shoulders sagged. He put the pieces together.

"Well fuck me running. You owe me now, mate. Owe me big."

"I'm good for it, you know that," Saul assured his friend.

He waved to George, who honestly looked far more interested in his work now he knew more of the backstory than practically anyone else in the Agency. Working the keyboard like a pro, he simply nodded as Saul led Jenn out of the building.

He paused when they were halfway down the street. Need rode him hard. He lifted Jenn's knuckles to his mouth and kissed them lovingly.

"Preston is calling in some favours, finding out what's really going on. This seems to be blowing out of control. That couple who we spotted before everything went to hell? Well, they're internal investigators, the go-to team if something isn't adding up or things are going bad. They seem connected to Chelsea and David's mission, whatever that is. Preston assured me the Dublin office is containing Vincent and Graeme and neither will breathe the air as free men again."

Jenn let out a long, deep sigh, as if a weight had been lifted from her. He couldn't help but feel pleased, proud of himself even though he'd not had a hand in either man's arrest. She remained silent, waiting for him to finish.

"I don't want you near this, you've already been exposed to too much danger," he continued. "So when we were offered a paid week away...I couldn't turn it down."

Jenn smiled beautifully at him, her whole face lighting up and making his heart pound.

"I don't care about whatever else is going on, not unless it involves you. Do you want to be a part of it? This mission? I can keep my head down if you want to stay and—"

"No, no, babe," he cut her off gently. His heart filled with love at her offer. "You're incredibly generous, thank you, but no. I'd much rather spend the next week wrapped up with you somewhere warm and cosy. I want to spend time with you. In some ways I know you better than anyone else alive, but in others there's still so much more to discover."

"I could say the exact same about you," she chuckled as they continued to where he'd parked the car. "I'm not going to complain if we spend a few weeks, or even years, in each other's pockets."

His heart sang with that knowledge. Saul stopped again so he could wrap his arms around her, draw her body tightly against his and kiss her passionately. His cock twitched to life, eager and willing to sink into her a million times and more—he didn't think he could ever get enough of her.

They were both breathless when he finally pulled away. Dipping his head so he could kiss the tip of her nose, he then moved his arm to rest across her shoulders. He tightened his hold on her, knew that he would never let her go. Together, they walked down the street.

Epilogue

Jenn woke slowly, drowsily. Through the open window a weak ray of sun struggled to peek through the clouds. The soft crash of the waves and scent of salt hung on the air. Opening one eye, she gazed around the now familiar room. As he'd promised, Saul had arranged everything and had whisked her off to the Isle of Wight only hours after they'd left the Agency.

That had been three days ago now. They'd forced themselves to leave the small cottage he'd rented, for ice cream or an intimate, romantic dinner or just a stroll along the sand. None of their trips had lasted long, though. Neither could keep their hands off each other. There were too many fantasies to explore.

Fantasies, she mused to herself. She grinned, stretched luxuriously and enjoyed the chance to take the initiative. Until now, Saul had always woken before her. His wicked mind had found any number of pleasurable ways to drag her away from her dreams and into the present. Now it was time for her to return the favour.

'...I want to suck your cock deeply into my mouth...feel you fucking down my throat... I want to know what it would be like to be possessed by you in my pussy and up my arse...'

Recalling her words from days ago, she felt renewed and refreshed. Determined. Saul had finger-fucked her in the arse the night before, stretched her tiny inner walls. Soaked with her own cream, his digit slick with copious lubricant, he'd driven her wild with pleasure. She'd come harder than she had known possible, screaming his name and clutching at him like he was some devilish god.

Moving carefully, not wanting to wake her gorgeous, sleeping lover, Jenn reached over him and quietly eased open the top bedside drawer. She removed the lubricant and a vibrator they'd packed from her stash of toys. This time she wouldn't let him talk her out of it. Jenn knew she was ready, damn near desperate, to feel what it would be like to have Saul plundering her arse.

It was time.

After placing the device and bottle of oil near Saul's pillow, Jennifer drew back the covers and scooted down the bed. She straddled Saul and took a moment to drink in the picture. She bent and warmly kissed his relaxed shaft. It immediately stirred at her touch. She ran her lips lightly over it, not wanting to jolt her lover awake but bring him out. He groaned, shifting his legs restlessly as his cock hardened.

Enticed, Jenn flicked her tongue out, tasting him as her heart sped with excitement. Saul's cock lengthened, thickened, and she took him into her mouth, suckling on him like a favourite treat. He moaned again and this time he fisted his hand into her hair, wrapping the long strands around his palm and urging her on.

Eagerly now, she started sucking him harder, moving her head and swallowing more of him. She lifted her fingers to stroke the skin of his sac, his balls tightening as his arousal grew. His cock was thick in her mouth now, a truly impressive morning wood.

"Babe," his voice was husky, laden with sleep and need.

She murmured, unable to speak around the swollen shaft stuffed inside her mouth.

Saul thrust his hips up, pressing deeper. Feeling deliciously ravished, she groaned her approval, sliding her free hand between her legs to stroke her aching clit. She caressed herself, spreading her cream slickly around her lips as she wallowed in him fucking her mouth.

"I'm too close, babe. I have to...ah..." Saul groaned and shuddered as he came down her throat.

Greedily she drank his seed as he shot into her with long bursts. Panting hard, Saul fell back onto the mattress.

Feeling pleased with herself, Jenn licked her lips. She relished the taste of him and savoured the salty muskiness of his cum. Jenn crawled up his body in a lithe, paced move. She felt powerful, feminine and desirable, she crawled up his body, kissing his lips for the first time that morning.

"That was a lovely teaser," he murmured.

"I decided it was time I got a chance to perform the morning greeting," she teased.

Saul stroked the tips of his fingers down the line of her back. She shivered, though not from the cool nip of the crisp air. Jenn couldn't believe she'd ever get tired of him, his touch or the magic they could create between them.

"You're perfect." Saul placed a string of kisses down her neck.

"There's more," she promised. "I want you to fuck me. In my arse."

She could feel Saul's heart hammer. She rested a hand over his chest, loving the proof of him so vital and strong beneath her.

"I might need a moment," he warned her.

Jenn shimmied over his body, decadently rubbing herself against him. She felt the first faint stirrings in his groin and stroked her hands over the smooth hardness of his delicious pectoral muscles.

"I'm sure I can give you incentive."

Loving the chance to thoroughly explore every inch of his body, she licked and kissed him everywhere possible. When Saul moved to clasp her hips, draw his half-hard shaft flush against her slick lips, she twisted teasingly out of reach.

"I'm taking my time, you wanted a moment or two." She laughed.

"Babe, I didn't mean for you to drive me wild," he groaned.

She could tell from his tone he was more resigned than upset. She chuckled again and went back to her languid play.

She shrieked with laughter when Saul finally lost his patience. His cock was thick, hard and fully erect. He was more than ready. Saul flipped them on the bed, kissing her with such heat and passion he stole her breath. She moaned, arching up into him.

"Please, Saul," she pleaded. "I really want this and I'm burning for you right now. Fuck my arse."

Saul drew her close. He gazed deeply into her eyes and lowered his hand, caressing his fingers over her slick lips. Drenched, she couldn't deny the truth of her aching for him. Turning his head, he grinned when he spotted the lube and vibrator.

Saul lifted his other hand, eased her face up to him and kissed her. Stroking her clit with his fingers, teasing her until she thought she'd ignite, Jennifer was panting hard, wriggling against him and gasping with need as he pulled back.

"Fuck it," he groaned. "I want this even more than you. Babe, you're magnificent."

Saul guided her so she supported herself on her hands and knees in the classic doggy style. She turned to watch over her shoulder as he squirted the gel onto his shaft, then smeared it until he gleamed.

When his fingers were slick, he spread her arse cheeks, exposed her tiny entrance and stroked her wetly. Nerves sizzled and energy arched the length of her body. Jenn curled her toes in reaction and her breaths came faster.

"Open for me, babe," Saul crooned.

She took a deep breath, swallowed the burning hunger urging her to demand he take her now, now, now and tried to embrace the need building inside her stomach.

Finally she felt the exquisite but still painful sensation of his fingers breaching her, she cried out. Despite the slick lubricant making his passage easier, and the anal-play he'd performed previously, he still seemed large, too big to fit within her. The searing intensity was no longer there, though. She knew she could accommodate him with time and finesse.

He pumped in and out, smoothing more gel inside her. This time pleasure swamped her quicker than before. The knot in her stomach grew, her nipples ached and she needed to stimulate her clit with just the right pressure. Flames of pleasure unfurled inside her stomach, licking their way up her torso, across her breasts and down to her hungry pussy.

"Oh yeah, you're nearly there," he murmured.

Jenn opened her eyes when he pressed the vibrator into her cunt in a deep, smooth stroke. Saul crouched over her, his dick rock-hard and jutting up proudly. The toy was one of her favourites, slender but long and made of smooth fibreglass so it was unyielding. It had a twisting bottom to change the speeds as needed.

"I've got this," she panted. Jenn took the vibrator and angled it so it could penetrate her shallowly but stimulate her clit. Jenn groaned as Saul removed his fingers from her arse. She pumped the vibrator to compensate for the loss.

She burned with need.

Turning her head, she watched Saul's face as he looked at her. He spread her cheeks, exposing her anus to his gaze. He slowly, finally, guided his shaft to her entrance. She couldn't see it, but she could feel the warm, swollen head push at her passage.

For a moment she panicked.

No way in fucking hell will that fit.

Her imagination ran wild, positive that his cock was along mammoth proportions and he'd rip her open pushing in. There was pressure, and pain, and she almost told him to stop. Frigging herself with the vibrator, she nibbled down on her bottom lip, determined to keep the words inside.

There was a sliding sensation. Saul exhaled as he glided into her in a long, slick motion.

It was a penetration like nothing she'd felt before. Every one of her senses heightened. Once again she became aware of the salty tang in the air, the sounds of the waves crashing onto the shore and their panting breaths. The bed beneath her hands and knees was soft and warm from their bodies.

And Saul. Inside her, surrounding her.

Holy fucking heavens, he's thick.

And enormous.

And deeply possessing every inch of her arse.

Time seemed to freeze. Saul didn't move. Jenn used the vibrator with shaky, twitchy thrusts that was more instinct than her brain sending out any messages. As if a switch had been thrown, her brain screamed into gear. Pleasure and pain overwhelmed her, crashed through her system like someone had decided to turn the music up.

She canted her hips back, pushing deeper onto his thick cock, plunging him further inside her.

Saul groaned like she was killing him. He cupped his hands over her hips, angling her then he pushed harder. Until that moment Jennifer had thought him fully lodged inside her channel. She'd been wrong. He filled her deeper. And deeper again.

Her heart hammered. Her throat and mouth felt like they were full of him.

It was wild. Intense. Frightening and absolutely bloody gorgeous.

Jenn never wanted it to end.

"Yes! Fucking hell, yes. Saul. More. Harder. Please."

It took her a moment to realise those words were falling from her, that she cried and wailed at him for everything. Energy zinged through her. Feeling reborn, she moved the vibrator with a frenzied motion, stimulating her clit and filling her pussy with a glorious feeling.

Hungrily her body clamped down on both shafts. She'd read about the intensity of double penetration, but never, ever in her wildest fantasies could she have believed how earth-shatteringly good it could have been.

An instant addict, she could only plead.

Saul went mad. His dark eyes blazed, his features looked like he was on the edge of ecstasy. Jenn tried to focus on him, on giving him everything she could in return, but all too soon the force of their lovemaking took her over. Her body shuddered, clenched him tightly and sent her over the edge.

She cried out, the orgasm blinding in its intensity.

Jenn forgot about the vibrator, the bed or keeping her balance, only the racking jolts shooting through her body and detonating in her pussy and arse registered in her mind. Dimly a part of her brain was aware of Saul bellowing, clenching his hands over her hips in a tight grip she knew should be painful but could only add to her enjoyment of the moment.

She felt his cock plunge into her, slamming within her tight passage. Despite the force he used, it made her gleeful to see the clear loss of control she'd pushed him to. He seemed unaware of his surroundings, focused completely on the momentous climax driving between them.

And then the wave of her orgasm washed away. Bliss and exhaustion vied for place and her limbs shook, no longer able to hold her up. Saul wrapped his arm around her waist and together they collapsed onto the mattress, him spooning her back close to his chest, his cock still lodged inside her body.

The air seemed full of their gasping, ragged breaths. Jenn laughed, caught somewhere between shocked ecstasy and a somewhat hysterical afterburn.

Nothing on earth could have prepared her for that.

Saul cradled her body and eagerly she snuggled back to him. It could have been one minute or ten, but finally she turned, cupped his face and kissed him tenderly.

"I love you," she murmured. "More than you will ever know."

"And I love you, babe. Always," he replied.

She could see the unwavering truth in his dark gaze.

Sated beyond measure, she cuddled close to her lover and drew in the clean, masculine scent of his skin with just a hint of the salty tang of his sweat. Jenn closed her eyes, pressed her ear to his chest and listened to the sound of his heart, happier than she could have ever believed.

UNEARTHED
TREASURE

Chapter One

Chelsea Atchison cast a brief look at her partner as she swiped her security pass to open the 'Employee Only' door. David Greer lifted an unsteady hand and tugged a stray lock of his shoulder-length hair behind his ear, his face reflecting the same confusion and surprise she felt.

The lock beeped and she depressed the handle. Brushing her long, dark brown curls away from her face she hurried through the door. She held it open until David Greer also passed through.

He shut the door behind them, the lock snicking audibly.

Her heart hammered, though she tried not to outwardly betray her concern.

So far their plans had turned totally to shit.

"What the hell happened out there?" she asked with a vague wave at the enormous main foyer of the National Gallery of London — where they'd just left. "None of this was supposed to happen. It sounded like a rocket launcher went off, and damned if the whole front façade of the building isn't decimated.

We've been planning for this afternoon for almost eighteen months, and now, mere hours from our goal, everything goes wrong."

"If by going wrong you mean half the city's police force are now likely on their way, yes, I think it's clear something is amiss," David replied.

Chelsea halted in the middle of the long corridor they had been hurrying through. Annoyed by the part sarcastic, part amused lilt to her partner's tone she pressed her hands to her hips and glared at him.

Of medium height and lithe build, it was only when one looked into those warm brown, steady eyes that David's intelligence and solid strength could be seen. Chelsea had trusted him from the moment she'd got a real, lasting look into his gaze. But it had been the sporadic flicker of a smile that helped soften his features. That, coupled with his lush, shoulder-length, medium brown hair got her heart pattering faster than usual.

David would never be a cover model, or sinfully handsome, but he more than revved her engines and set her breath racing from a casual glance.

"Don't you take that tone with me. I played my part to the letter. I warned you that woman Jennifer was trouble the moment you told me she'd seen you bury the box with the spare security card and blueprints in it. Anyone would be curious after having seen that. I'm surprised it took so long for her and that Agency fellow Saul to put the pieces together."

"You agreed we should keep the London branch of the Agency out of this. I explained the situation to you. I never lied."

Chelsea sighed. She could just make out the sound of approaching sirens. They both kept walking, though more calmly now.

"I know. But we've come so far, we're so close to hearing what the smugglers consider the main goal—Phase Two to their plan."

"We'll get there," David insisted in a low tone. "If you want to back out, to call it quits—"

"Bite your tongue," she replied.

Chelsea turned her head to look over her shoulder at David. He watched her carefully, his dark brown eyes serious. She knew his lithe build was deceptive, he didn't look anywhere near as physically strong as she knew he was. Brown hair fell in a soft curtain to graze his shoulders and frame his angular face. Normally she loved hearing him speak, the faint lilt of his accent reminding her of home and warmth—of comfort.

She reached out and surprised them both by taking his hand, threading their fingers together.

"We're a team," she said firmly. "There is not a person on this planet more fierce or stubborn than the two of us. I know we've had our problems, particularly when we were first partnered for this mission. But over the last year and a half I've come to rely on your instincts, I listen to your judgements and we make all our decisions together. We're partners. Equals. Unless you're wanting to back out of this mission I don't want to hear another word about giving up, especially not for something as insulting as you wanting to protect me."

"No one is more important to me than you," he said with a simple, brutal honesty. Chelsea smiled, certain there would be some joke or additional comment coming on the heels of his statement, but David simply watched her, seemingly waiting for her response. Her smile faded. She realised he meant the words exactly as he'd said them.

"David," she stammered, surprised, pleased, excited. A whirl of emotions grew inside her as she understood that the growing attraction she was feeling for this man was reciprocated. Heavy boots sounded from behind them.

They both turned to glance back, then simultaneously broke into a run.

"Damn it," Chelsea cursed. "This is not the fucking time. I just can't catch a break with you, can I?"

"If it wasn't this it would be something else," David replied with a wry grin. "The rest of the smuggling team, armed assault agents, something."

"This conversation isn't over," she promised him. "But maybe we should get somewhere secure first."

Chelsea swiped her security pass beside one of the offices. It was a medium-sized room shared by three of the Gallery's employees and for the most part was unremarkable. What made this particular office of interest to them was the fact that it had a small window looking out onto the back gardens.

David hefted a chair and threw it through the glass. It shattered with an almighty crash. Chelsea wasn't fazed by the cacophony that followed — she knew everyone would be busy with the burning wreckage over at the front of the Gallery. She doubted anyone would even notice the damage until they were long gone.

"Security systems are all down," Chelsea recalled with relief. "Since one of those idiots decided to shoot the hell out of the front of the Gallery every alarm has been blaring for nearly five minutes now, hence the police. Was that really a rocket launcher which they'd used to destroy one of the columns out front?"

"Remember how Thaddeus kept on boasting he could get his hands on anything — even a tank or a single person rocket launcher?" David reminded her.

Groaning, Chelsea nodded. Thaddeus was one of the more unstable men in the crew they were working undercover in. She realised he must have been given free rein to prove his boasts. She could well imagine how the pieces fitted together, now. Chelsea climbed onto the sill of the window, making sure the glass panes were all removed and wouldn't cut her as she climbed through.

"Who let Thaddeus have his party?"

Chelsea waited on the ledge while David climbed up beside her.

"I believe it was Phillipe," David replied. Chelsea groaned again. Kent Phillipe was the very paranoid leader of the crew. Something about the deal had definitely turned sour if he'd got an itchy trigger finger this late in the game.

"Let's go," she said. Together they jumped out of the window, falling about ten feet onto soft grass. They both landed smoothly and walked quickly away from the Square. Lights flashed everywhere, dozens of ambulances, police cars and emergency response vehicles having converged around the Gallery, with still more arriving and blocking traffic.

Dressed in a navy, pencil-slim skirt and suit jacket, Chelsea could pass for any regular businesswoman walking the streets. David had nondescript black slacks and a leather jacket on. Not concerned in the least about blending in, they moved out onto the street.

David threw his arm around Chelsea's shoulder. She tossed her long curls back and hugged him in return, her hand lightly resting on his waist. They walked easily in time with each other, their bodies leaning close together, the very image of lovers out for a romantic stroll.

When they were most of the way down the street, Chelsea spoke again.

"Should we call Phillipe? Or McIlroy?"

"You'd risk checking in with the Agency?" David replied, sounding surprised.

"He is our boss." She chuckled before growing more serious. "If we've possibly been compromised then the Dublin branch needs to know what's going on, and what we've learnt. Even though we don't know their final target they might have time to discover it some other way."

"There wasn't another way to breach this group," David reminded her. "That's why we were called in. Look, we've been undercover together, breaking who knows how many laws for eighteen months. One, maybe two more weeks and we'll be out and free, finally. I'd like to see it through. I know you would too."

Chelsea sighed but nodded. He knew her so well, better than anyone else alive.

"Hey," he said softly, pulling her close. Chelsea rested her head on his shoulder, soaking up the support he offered her unconditionally. "Something's bugging you, what is it?"

She pressed her lips together at first, not wanting to speak the words aloud, to admit the growing knot of tension and feelings in the base of her stomach. But this was David. For more than a year now she'd had no one else to turn to, no one she had been able to rely on, speak to with any semblance of honesty or just be with. She could trust him with everything and anything. Most important of all, she'd come to love this man, to need him on every level and crave his presence more than an addict requires their drug of choice.

She loved him. Deeply.

Chelsea needed to be honest with him, no matter how ugly *that* might turn out to be.

"I've enjoyed this," she started hesitantly. The words grew inside her until they flowed out of her, a wound finally lanced. "I love thinking on my feet, outsmarting the bad guys, feeding information back to the Agency and watching this smugglers network slowly crumble. I won't lie, it's been bloody hard in a number of places, but I've loved having you as my partner. Despite our struggles sometimes, we work magnificently together. I'm worried when this is said and done they'll split us up. Or assign us to some dumbass, boring analyst job, or stupid bodyguarding protective duty. I couldn't handle that. Or being separated from you."

"I'd leave the Agency rather than leave you," David said calmly. "But let's not get ahead of ourselves. There's plenty more to do here, and you know what the world is like, there will always be a need for people like us. One thing I can guarantee, that I can promise you without a doubt. As long as you want it, we will be together. I don't ever want to be apart from you, either. You're the hidden treasure I found on this mission, not the jewels we've helped recover, not the stolen artworks or gold bullion bars. You."

They'd entered a quiet alley behind a row of boutique stores. Chelsea paused, her gaze searching David's. She reached out a hand and brushed his soft hair behind his ear. Now she could peer into his speaking, dark eyes.

"You mean that?" she whispered. "Because if you're talking pretty or just trying to get into my knickers I will gut you like a fish. That's a promise. Don't mess with me, Dave."

"Damn you have the most beautiful eyes." He chuckled. "They sparkle like sapphires when you're mad, or passionate. I've never met anyone with deeper blue eyes than you."

Chelsea raised an eyebrow, knowing in her heart he wouldn't tease her like this, waxing lyrical about her damn eyes, if he didn't love her as much as she had come to love him. Still. She needed the words.

"I love you. I adore you. I'd break a million more laws and flee this country should it be necessary to keep you. And you know how attached to this soil I am."

Chelsea indeed knew David well enough by now to know he meant those words. She cupped his jaw, loving the silky feel of his long hair as it caressed her skin. Tilting her head up, she pressed her body against his, pushing him back into the brick wall of the alley, and kissed him passionately.

They'd shared a few simple kisses, mostly when keeping up the pretence of being lovers. This intimacy blew all the others out of the water. His lips were soft, so tender they seemed sinful to her. He opened his mouth and she slipped her tongue inside, relishing the taste of him.

His mouth was hot, dark and moist. He stroked his tongue over hers. Chelsea moaned, her pussy throbbing with need. She felt David's arms close around her hips, angling her so his thigh thrust between her legs. She rode him now, eagerly seeking more friction as pleasure shot through her body.

Their kiss deepened as he moved his hands over her clothing. He sought her secret sweet spots, tenderly touching where he could reach. She lifted her hand to touch the edge of his jaw, then lightly stroked his skin. She felt him tremble and it sent a feeling of power over her.

Chelsea sprang away as a car turned down the alley, interrupting them.

She cast a look at David. His eyes had darkened. His lips were full and red from their passion. She lifted a finger to her own lips, finding them damp and puffy from the intensity of their kiss. Her breaths came fast and her need for him blossomed—a desperate craving raced through her. She needed to touch and taste all of him, to feel David's thick cock as it thrust inside her every opening.

They both pressed against the side of the alley to allow the car to pass them. Afterwards, they glanced at one another. Chelsea grinned. They both acted like a pair of teenagers caught necking behind the proverbial shed.

"So I guess we should call Phillipe, ask him what the hell was going on. I can't think of why he let Thaddeus loose like that," she said.

"I've got a few ideas," David admitted. "But they're all conjecture. I agree we should—"

Chelsea's phone sounded, the upbeat tone interrupting his words. Frowning, she dipped a hand into her work satchel and pulled it out. She raised an eyebrow at David.

"McIlroy," she said, the single word not needing any further explanation. Opening the phone, she tilted it. David bent his head so he could also hear the man's responses while she carried on the conversation.

She spoke into the receiver in the firm, clipped tone she reserved for their boss when she figured they were going to get yelled at. It occurred far more often than she'd ever have thought possible. "Hello?"

"Atchison. Fucking hell! You're going to age me a decade before you and Greer wrap up this mission. Why am I hearing initial reports about a rocket launcher decimating the front pillars of the National Gallery down there? Have you and Greer no sense of discretion? Decorum? I should let the London branch have you both with my blessing, or get them to forcibly drag you both back up here to mountain goat-herding duties. What the hell is going on down there?"

"The rocket launcher wasn't us," she replied when McIlroy paused for breath. "Phillipe let Thaddeus loose, and... Well, the man's been boasting of his connections and probably felt he had a point to prove."

"What made them go early?" McIlroy questioned, sounding like he already had begun to calm down.

"We're not sure yet. We've only just escaped ourselves. There were...a few complications."

"Like what?"

"A woman saw David burying some of the evidence we've collected. Nothing big, small stuff, but she apparently is dating, or connected somehow with, Saul Haslen—he's Agency here in London. We weren't aware of it until just now. He's been sniffing around, and between them they've made some waves. We're not certain how it all ties together yet, but that's what we were going to work on once we reconnect with Phillipe."

"Sounds like it's getting messy."

David rolled his eyes at her.

"It's nothing we can't handle, Sir." His soft brogue made the words sound particularly respectful.

Truly, over the last year and a half they'd meshed together perfectly as a team, playing off each other's strengths and weaknesses. Without conscious thought, Chelsea had outlined the bad news, explaining the reality of the situation in her blunt, straightforward manner. Now David could smooth their path over and sweet-talk their boss into doing things the way they wanted to.

It wasn't a guaranteed method of success, but had worked well for them in the past. With luck, now would be no different.

Chelsea blew a silent kiss to David, relieved she could always rely on him.

"The London office is going to be annoyed we've all but stepped on their feet here," McIlroy warned them.

"The smuggling has always been outside their jurisdiction," David pointed out smoothly. "Until Phillipe needed to expand his crew and set their sights on someplace as impenetrable as the National Gallery, their actions would have never been more than a blip of minor curiosity to London. Remind them of that. And also point out the only reason they're getting interested is one of their own, Haslen, is acting macho and protective of his woman. This is our case—we've put almost two years of our life into it. Neither of us will appreciate having it stolen from us at this late stage."

"And we're well established here," Chelsea added. "We're on some rocky ground, sure, but we're in. No one else would be given admittance if we're pulled now. The crew would just make do."

"I'll try to hold them off," McIlroy said, though he clearly wasn't thrilled with the idea. "When can you report back? I'm sure my phone will be ringing nonstop as soon as others are made aware of what's happening here. I'll need something more than the promise of autonomy we usually get."

"Get London to give us space to do our job," David said in a soothing tone. "We'll reconnect with the crew, act all outraged and get some answers. We were supposed to have the primary target by now so we can't be in the dark much longer."

"Watch your arses," McIlroy grunted.

Chelsea threw a laughing glance at David. Heat bloomed between them. There had been a connection growing steadily over the last few months as they'd both toed closer to the line between flirting and something deeper. Having only one another to rely on had forged an unbreakable bond. Sometimes she felt David was the only person who knew her, who understood her actions and could second-guess her thoughts.

With David in her life, it had changed only for the better. She hated the thought that they might be separated. Knowing now that he feared that as much as her helped ease her concern. Attraction flared between them, addictively potent. She couldn't—wouldn't—pretend anymore that she didn't want him, that he didn't make her pussy wet every time he stared at her with his dark eyes.

She could no longer pretend she didn't notice the hungry way he watched her, or that she didn't feel the exact same way.

"We'll be fine," Chelsea said into the phone, though her words weren't only for McIlroy. "We'll be in touch when we have the details for Phase Two."

McIlroy hung up. She closed the phone then replaced it in her satchel.

"What now?" she asked. Her gaze rested on David, asking him more than how they would proceed with their mission from there.

David reached out one pale hand. He lightly caressed her curls, stroking her with a tenderness that touched her very soul.

"Are you sure you want to be with me to confront them?" His voice was husky. She wondered what he was thinking—if it was even half as naughtily sexy as she imagined. "If they've made us...not necessarily as agents, but even just as not truly part of their cause then...well...it would kill me if they hurt you. If they know exactly how much I love you they could use that knowledge to disastrous effect."

She tilted her head to the side, enjoying the way he brought a hand up to cup her face. "I could say the same thing to you," she replied. "If they threatened you, hurt you because I held out on them, I'd never forgive myself. I'd tell them whatever they wanted to know, betray everything we both believe in. I couldn't sit by and let you be harmed. This is a far more dangerous game we're playing now."

"I'd never let it get that far," he promised solemnly. "We're both so stubborn, I'm sure we could get out of any scrape we fall into. But that doesn't mean I like the thought of you walking into what could very well be a trap."

She grinned.

"You think I'd let you walk into that meeting without me to guard your ass?" she shook her head. "We're well matched when it comes to independence and pig-headedness. There's no chance in hell you're going in there alone. I'm fond of your ass, and other more intriguing parts of that well-honed body of yours. I'm coming with you, end of story."

"I treasure you," he said huskily.

And I, you, she was about to say, but his face loomed over hers for a split second before they kissed once again. Hungrily she devoured him. They roamed their hands over one another. Chelsea ached to discover as much of him as possible. It seemed that David sought her secrets just as eagerly. She groaned, there was only so much they could do with their clothes on. The sound of a car horn had them both instantly whirling apart, standing shoulder to shoulder as they faced off against the enemy.

They were faced with a cherry red, sporty little hatchback, driven by a young woman. She gesticulated with her hands for them to move out of the way.

Chelsea snickered, amused at how they could both be so on edge, but still find their attraction so overwhelming they could lose all sense of time and space. She thought she heard the driver shout "Get a room!" but with the window closed she couldn't be certain.

"You're intoxicating," Chelsea chided David as they continued down the alley towards their parked car. "I'm going to get shot in the back because my entire focus revolves around you and tasting you whenever you so much as look at me."

"For weeks now I've done nothing but fantasise about thrusting deeply into your every orifice," David replied. "It's been...difficult, shall we say."

"Difficult?" She shot him a glance, struggling not to laugh at his understatement. "I wish we had time, but the longer we wait, the worse it will look for us."

David nodded as they came up to the car.

"Agreed. But later?"

"Later," she promised, the word a vow, an oath.

"Make the call," he said as he unlocked the doors.

She slid into the passenger seat. Chelsea placed her satchel at her feet and snapped on her seatbelt. After pulling her phone out, she dialled Kent Phillipe's number. David sat next to her and started the car. As he pulled away, she organised her thoughts, tried to block the intimate awareness of the man so close to her in the confines of the car.

Her skin tingled. Her pussy throbbed with hunger. But she pushed all that away, knowing she needed to hit exactly the right note with the mid-level smuggler.

Chelsea knew she needed to sound outraged, offended and hurt, but not overdo it and seem too dramatic. She needed to prove she could keep a cool head when things went wrong. Similarly she knew they had to lay enough blame at Phillipe's door and act the part of wronged innocents, but still prove that they were willing to complete the mission and continue onto whatever Phase Two happened to be.

It would be a delicate balance. She needed to concentrate.

"Atchison," Kent answered. "You with Greer?"

"Yes, we're both here," she replied. "What the fuck is going on? This was not in our plan, Phillipe. I wasn't even close to having things set up. We weren't going through with this until later tonight. I'd barely even entered the Gallery when all hell broke loose. You could have compromised me, blown this whole thing out of the water. I need some answers—"

"Cool it, things went exactly according to plan," Phillipe snapped, cutting her off mid-sentence.

Chelsea cast a curious glance to David. He looked equally surprised and shook his head to indicate he had no idea what the man was talking about.

"I don't know what kind of game you're playing—" she began hotly, getting annoyed now.

Again he cut her off. "Come back to base, you and David both. We'll discuss it there."

Before she could get a word further, Kent hung up on her.

She pressed her lips together, annoyed, frustrated and concerned. Kent Phillipe was not some elegant gentleman with impeccable manners. But he had never spoken so briskly to her, or with such disdain, either. She worried that maybe they really were compromised.

"Last chance," David reiterated. She shook her head firmly.

"No, I want to stand with you on this," she repeated. "Not just to protect you, but I don't run from slime like him. If a few harsh words scared me off I'd never recover my pride. Sometimes, I have so much fun with this sort of work I forget it's not all sunshine and laughter, that batting my eyelashes and wiggling my arse isn't always the answer."

"I dunno," mused David, a wicked gleam in his eye. "I bet if you wriggled your arse at me there's very little it couldn't answer for."

She laughed, leaned over and pressed a kiss to his cheek.

"I'll remember that," she warned him.

David laid his hand on her thigh, the connection sizzling between them. "I hope you do."

Chapter Two

They'd arrived at a dingy business park. A long row of factories, many of them evidently abandoned, sat on an enormous concrete slab. Kent Phillipe had organised for their crew to use one of the empty warehouses as their main base of operations.

Chelsea and David crossed the street and made a beeline from the car to the hideout. Knowing they would be heavily scrutinised once they entered, and that only visual security was outside the building, she spoke quickly, moving her lips as little as possible. "Do you want to take the lead here, or should I?"

"I'll remain the quiet, observant security expert," David replied. "Besides, it was you they tapped initially to work with them. It would make more sense for you to be the more offended party here."

Casting him a quick, curious glance, Chelsea pondered his reply. They were a few hundred yards away when another reason he preferred to play the quiet, unobtrusive character in front of these people illuminated her mind.

"You're going to take the heat if they think we're traitorous," she said with an furious tone. For a moment she felt tempted to stop right where they were and argue this out with him. Common sense reared its head before she could literally jolt to a stop, but her fury was real.

"David, damn it, I'm not going to hang you out to dry, or let you do it to yourself. We're a team, remember? If you think—"

"Hush, love," David snapped. "If you raise your voice much more they'll be able to hear you from inside. We both have a right to be angry, that's easily explained, but if anyone is going to go down here it's me. Swear to me you'll cut me loose if it comes to that."

"I'll promise nothing of the sort," she said, beyond incensed. "I can handle anything these pansies throw at me, but I refuse, *refuse* to sit idly by while they hurt you. Stand or fall, David. We'll be doing it together."

David nodded, though his dark eyes flashed with barely suppressed temper. He didn't appear the least impressed by the ferocity of her response.

"Then I sincerely hope one or the both of us can talk ourselves out of whatever's going on."

They walked up to the entrance that had been carved out of the metal roller door. Chelsea dug a hand into her coat pocket and removed a small ring of keys. Selecting the correct one quickly, she inserted it into the lock, and after knocking, opened the door. She went in first, forcing herself to calm down and think positively.

She'd talked herself out of some very tight corners. Words often came easily to her. More than one other agent had been astonished by her flair for discourse. She had a deeply curious brain and held a large range of interests, which kept her ability to adapt to situations keen. Add on her verbose nature and a substantial vocabulary, and some would say she was born for this sort of thing.

Well, being either an agent or a swindler.

Half the time Chelsea wondered if the two weren't extremely closely linked. The line between each task frequently blurred for her.

Chelsea entered the cavernous room first, though David remained right behind her. She didn't need to be psychic to know that, should they be attacked outright, he would push her aside and take the brunt of the fire. Keeping her balance on the balls of her feet, she remained sharply aware, ready to dive and cover David's body with her own should it come to it.

Three men stood in tight formation in the middle of the room, next to the trestle tables they'd set up weeks ago. Just as they'd been when she'd last seen them a few days ago, the tables were covered with blueprints, schematics and hand-copied routes of security rounds, along with dossiers of the guards who were to have been on duty tonight.

The set-up reminded Chelsea of what she imagined a war room would have looked like back in the day. Markers were laid out to indicate motion sensors, cameras and exits where the guards who smoked were known to pause for ten minutes to enjoy a quiet break midway through their rounds.

The fact that the area hadn't been cleaned up gave her strength. If Phillipe were cutting his losses or disbanding their crew, chances were that all this paraphernalia would be long gone. Things still didn't look good for her or David, but a flicker of hope caught fire in her chest.

Over six foot, slender and with a head full of black hair, Phillipe looked more like the French aristocrat he pretended to be than the fixer and criminal he was. The leader of the group, he stood in the middle of the three men, his arms crossed over his chest as he waited, clearly impatient. To his left stood a shorter, reed-thin man dressed head to foot in black.

Luke Calloway was a Brit through and through, with a mixed accent that varied depending on his mood and circumstance. Chelsea had decided after a few months that Luke had risen from a poor background. When he became very excited or extremely annoyed, his smooth, Eton-style accent disintegrated into a choppier mesh of lower-class slang. He was the best thief she'd ever encountered. Had he not so clearly lacked empathy and a modicum of common decency she'd have been tempted to try to recruit him for the Agency.

Thaddeus Brown stood on Phillipe's other side. Taller than Calloway but shorter than Phillipe he looked like an ex-rugby player. Brawny, thick-necked with closely cut, pale blond hair, he was their weapons master and ammunition expert. Anything to do with guns, knives or bullets was his domain. More than once he'd bragged about the time he'd taken a tank for a 'test drive' five hundred miles out into the country to blow up an ex-girlfriend's summer house. The first time she'd heard the story Chelsea had laughed, thinking it a wonderful joke. After spending a few months with the man, she no longer considered it funny — or a lie.

It took a while to notice, but there was a craziness in Thaddeus' eyes. Subtle enough to not recognise at first, third or even tenth glance, it was prominent enough that he couldn't hide it forever.

Although Thaddeus scared her, being the stubborn, independent woman she was, Chelsea refused to show it or let it affect her in any way. The world was full of craziness. Thaddeus was more volatile and dangerous than many men, but she knew there were worse out there.

That didn't mean she relaxed her guard around him. Not ever.

Chelsea paused a few feet away from the three men. She tilted her chin and placed her hands on her hips. David stood directly behind her elbow, only a tiny distance behind her, clearly showing she was in charge, but that he supported her fully.

Tension crackled in the air as they silently faced off.

Not wanting to make this a staring contest or a battle of wills for who could remain silent the longest, she shrugged her shoulders and decided to get on with things.

"Well?" she said sharply, her tone cutting through the air like a knife. "What the hell were you thinking? I assume that bloody rocket launcher was courtesy of you, Thaddeus. Do you realise, had you been a minute or two earlier, I'd have still been out front and you could have killed me? How, then, would you have got access internally into the Gallery? Or any new roster changes of the security shifts?"

Thaddeus grinned at her, a mocking, eager look crossing his face. His expression made Chelsea worry.

"I guess that's all moot now anyway, since every cop in central London is probably crawling over the area. Were you really trying to kill me? Or worse—have me arrested. I've only been on loan to the Gallery two months, I haven't activated any of my deletion or encryption files as yet, nor any of the fail safes I'll point out I spent months carefully inserting to remove all our tracks. If the police have enough wits they'll put it together sooner or later and I'll need to find myself a new identity. That shit costs dearly, you realise that, right?"

Chelsea drew herself taller, straightening her spine proudly and stared at Kent. She gauged that now was the time to remain silent since she'd said her opening piece. Kent's warm smile unsettled her. Her stomach rolled uneasily though she kept any such fear from her face.

If he's going to shoot me in the face or the gut now will be the time, she guessed in a flash of intuition.

Bracing herself, Chelsea held her ground, her chin tilted, her body tensed for the potential impact. Although she was quite worried, she refused to show even a smidgen of fear.

Phillipe burst out laughing.

The tension snapped, dissipated as if it had never been present in the first place. Phillipe clapped his hands together like a chortling goblin, anticipating his next nasty spell.

"Damn but you're gorgeous when you're angry. Your eyes snap this blue fire and your face flushes like a woman about to reach climax. It really is a sight to behold."

Relief had her tone lessening some of its bite, but she didn't have to pretend to still be seriously annoyed. That emotion was all too real.

"So there's a reason—other than seeing me mad, I mean—that you blew the hell out of the Gallery almost eight hours earlier than we'd planned?"

"Of course, Chelsea," Phillipe soothed her. He thrust his hands into the pockets of his coat and relaxed his posture. "I kept you in the dark because I didn't know I could trust you."

Fully expecting far more of an explanation than that cryptic sentence, Chelsea waited. When he said nothing further she waved a hand, gesturing for him to continue.

"That's it? Sorry I almost killed you, sorry we set every cop in the city racing to you, but it was a test?"

"I've worked with Thaddeus here and Luke on a number of other operations. I trust them. I know their strengths, weaknesses, where they can stand firm and what will make them crack. I only have Lawrence's assurances that you're reliable and good at what you do. Now, I trust Lawrence, he's never failed to connect me with the perfect partner for my crews yet, but I wasn't born yesterday. There's a certain reticence when such an important job means using someone I've never worked with before."

"That and the fact that you insisted on bringing in silent boy over there," Thaddeus added thickly, his tone showing disdain for David. "That hasn't helped any either."

Chelsea pressed her lips together. They'd had this argument in various forms a few times since they'd joined the crew many months ago.

"We've been over this," she said in a low tone, a warning in her voice. "You didn't have a security expert. The National Gallery is not some dodgy bank with standard items any fool on his first day can crack. My arse was on the line there. You needed an inside plant and I was your girl. I held up my part of the bargain, but we needed that extra edge and you know it. David is one of the best there is. We've covered this ground months ago. And again, it's all lost now because...because why? You wanted to test me somehow?"

"Oh, more than that, precious," Kent purred. "And don't worry, you and your man here passed with flying colours. As a side note, Thaddeus was watching you enter the Gallery. He had explicit instructions to wait until you were a safe distance inside. You were never really in any danger."

Chelsea merely lifted an eyebrow at this. She didn't think Phillipe was lying, but in truth it was impossible to tell for certain.

"Okay, so we passed, fantastic. That doesn't change the fact that the Gallery is now crawling with cops. Likely the Board of Directors will double or triple the number of patrols. Add onto that all the really sensitive and most expensive exhibits will be returned or moved into the vault—which we've already agreed is completely impenetrable—and so it doesn't matter that you're keeping secrets and we don't know what the actual target is. There's no way to get at it now."

"Oh ye of little faith," Phillipe intoned. He turned, gesturing that Chelsea and David should follow him. Thaddeus and Luke both moved when Phillipe did, heading for the work area and the five seats spread around the trestle tables.

Chelsea shot a quick glance to David. His features had been set in hard planes while they'd argued. Now the main event seemed over she could see he had relaxed, albeit only a tiny amount. None of the others could possibly have seen the minute tell-tale signs, but she did. She also agreed the imminent danger had passed. They were still on thin ice, but she felt that Phillipe had found whatever he had been searching for between them.

Kent paused a second until both Chelsea and David stepped forward. When he saw them move he turned and continued over to stand beside his usual seat at the head of the bench.

Thaddeus and Luke had already taken their seats. A gentleman to his core, David paused beside his seat as Chelsea drew the strap of her satchel over her head, placed the bag at her feet and sat. Only then did David also sit. Phillipe remained standing.

"In part you're completely right, Atchison," Kent said. His body appeared completely relaxed but Chelsea wasn't fooled. It was clear that David didn't believe the danger was completely passed either — his body remained alert and tense. Phillipe, in contrast, leaned onto his chair, one hand clasped around the backrest, one leg casually crossed in front of the other, the very picture of an indolent dandy of times past.

"The Gallery, as I'm sure you're aware, has a standard procedure for how to respond to such attacks like we performed today. Part of that is to ferry the most highly prized articles — those with mammoth insurance policies and delicate items on loan from notoriously volatile countries like Africa and the Middle East — and spirit them immediately away to be locked in the depths of the vault. As you so astutely pointed out, it's damn near impossible, not to mention impractical for our purposes, for us to attempt entrance into that area."

Chelsea nodded when Kent paused, seeming to want a response from her. After her acknowledgement he continued, "What interested us, however, was another section of this procedure, where it explains in detail how, while they do triple security, tighten patrols and go on a higher level of alertness, this is simultaneously their greatest flaw."

Phillipe's tone had turned decidedly smug now. Chelsea repeated his words in her head, looking for something she seemed to be overlooking. At first his meaning was too subtle to pick up on, but then the germ of an idea began to form.

"We're not after a high risk target," she surmised.

David didn't move so much as a hair beside her, so she couldn't understand why she had the distinct impression that he'd had a light-bulb moment go off in his brain. Not daring to risk a glance at him—they weren't free and clear just yet—she kept her focus upon Phillipe. Surprisingly, though, a part of her was perpetually aware of David, almost a sixth sense that remained drawn to her partner.

Making a mental note to examine that feeling in more depth later, Chelsea smiled when Kent gave her a small round of applause.

"Exactly, my girl." He beamed like she was his new prize student. "Yes, there will be more heightened security, and many more bodies roaming the corridors—but only selected corridors. Rounds through the larger exhibits will double, and adrenaline will have those poor sods trigger happy and itching to prove themselves and earn a bonus. But it will be focused upon all the well-known, far more expensive sections."

"That corridor housing the local Art College's award winners will be practically empty." Luke spoke for the first time that afternoon. "It won't be isolated or ignored, but they will be paying far less attention to it, and the rounds will be farther apart than usual."

"So by attacking early, heightening security and awareness, you've effectively now created less resistance for us to bypass in a couple of sections," Chelsea summarised. "That's pretty ballsy. Are you certain it worked?"

"We'll find out tonight," Kent answered with a smirk. He picked up two thin folders and tossed them down the table at her and David. Chelsea reached forward, David leaning at the same time to collect his.

"The Boss wants us to collect one of Cézanne's lesser known works. These are the details," Kent explained. "It's actually left over from last year's huge European Post-Impressionist exhibit. Most of the larger works have been returned and scattered, but the owner of this particular piece has been away sunning themselves in a small, tax-free island hideaway and gave permission for the Gallery to keep it for now. It's in the equivalent of a small, forgotten back corner."

"A Cézanne hidden away in the corner?" Chelsea repeated, hardly able to imagine it.

"It's one of his earlier works," Phillipe replied with a disinterested shrug. "Not in his prime. Regardless, it's one of the few sections we noticed where the lesser quality works are held and should be a fairly simple piece to acquire. It's why we attacked this morning to set this plan in motion."

"The Boss wants a second-rate, almost forgotten piece of art?" David spoke up for the first time. "Out of every piece inside the famous National Gallery he wants this? Why?"

Kent glared at David, his dislike for her partner clear to see.

"Does it matter? The money is good, the risk is now minimal. Maybe he likes Cézanne, or his Missus wanted one for her birthday. You'll get to meet him and that's what you've been angling for, right?"

"It's the only way to set up our own cell," David replied placidly.

"Oh that's right," Kent sneered. "Mr High and Mighty wants to be his own boss, only he doesn't have the connections or balls for it. You know, it's hard to trust you when you've never even pretended to want to be on this team. You're here to set out for yourself. And you wonder why I've got my suspicions about you?"

"Sometimes two personalities clash. It's a fact of life," David pointed out.

"Right. And I'm just your stepping stone to the next level up. Well, you seem to have attracted his attention. He mentioned you, specifically, last time we communicated. Seems the Boss was curious why you didn't kill that girl and save him the trouble."

Chelsea frowned, worried at the turn the conversation had suddenly taken. If it was about what she thought, this could be dangerous for them all.

"What girl?" she asked, playing dumb and hoping it was something else entirely.

"The pretty little blonde thing who saw him burying evidence related to this heist."

Tension knotted in her stomach for the first time. This was obviously what had been lurking in the background—the reason she hadn't been able to fully relax even after they'd been over the 'test' earlier that morning. Subconsciously at least she'd understood there was more to come.

If she were honest with herself, though, the real reason her belly was now tied in knots wasn't because Kent was again questioning their loyalty to their team and the mission. It was because the man's eyes rested solidly, unwavering upon David.

Chelsea didn't mind having to talk quickly, to unravel something seemingly unexplainable. In a twisted sense she got a lot of pleasure from doing just that—it was one of the reasons she loved espionage and her job in general. But knowing it was David, not she, who was now under the microscope had her breaking out into a cold sweat of fear for him.

Reminded of the mammoth handgun tucked away in her satchel, she reassured herself that this wasn't David's first day on the job. Just as she needed him to trust that she could handle herself, so too did she need to have unshakeable faith in him. She forced a smile to her face, carefully relaxing her posture in the seat to indicate not a single iota of concern.

It was one of the hardest things she'd ever had to do. The gut-deep instinct to leap to her partner's defence beat at her. Instead, she kept herself ready to spring into action should it all go to hell, while looking as if the two men were discussing the weather.

"What about her?" David asked in his calm, soft-toned way.

"You were compromised," Kent growled. "Now, I know you think you're hot shit, that you're ready for the big leagues. Somehow, though, I'd thought even you had enough brain cells rattling around that tiny head of yours to realise if someone catches you burying evidence, you do something about it. Something constructive and...permanent."

"Killing someone is a big deal," David replied after waiting a short pause. "I've found something so irreversible always creates more problems than it solves. Friends and family ask difficult questions. They hassle the local police until they dig deeper just to get them off their backs. Ex-lovers vow revenge and even mild-mannered people can become flaming furies when they feel they've been hard done by. I've found such permanent measures rarely end the matter there and the problem remains unsolved."

"But that's just my point. As far as I can see you aren't solving this 'problem' at all."

"On the contrary."

Chelsea shivered lightly as David's tone turned positively arctic. Kent's needling appeared to be getting beneath her partner's skin. She remained silent and didn't move, not wanting to make matters worse. It might be her personal bias, but she felt David had made a few good points and certainly seemed to be holding his own against their leader.

"I've been keeping close tabs on the woman," David continued. "Should she pose a genuine threat I'll deal with it."

"What were you doing burying such sensitive data, anyway?" Luke asked, stepping in for the minute.

David turned his attention to the other man. Thaddeus, Chelsea noticed, appeared extremely bored by the whole byplay. He repeatedly flipped a small throwing knife up and over. The blond man's lips moved as he appeared to count the number of rotations he could perform before needing to catch the knife in his palm.

"As I'm sure you're aware," David replied with an icy calm, "data like this is an investment. I'm certain we aren't the only team to have ever wanted such details. You don't destroy information like this. It has perpetual utility. Some people use bank vaults, others deposit boxes. I've heard of some who even prefer under abandoned houses or similar such places. I prefer to go to the middle of the boondocks and bury it. The chances of someone hunting it down are far smaller than anything else I just mentioned."

"Except this time someone was there," Kent snapped.

"Obviously more than one 'someone' was there," David pointed out harshly. "I saw those men who tried to kidnap her. I presume those were the amateurs you sent? They were easy to lose."

Kent pressed his lips together angrily but didn't say anything.

David nodded as if the man had admitted doing so. "I thought so. So you're prepared to hang me for not 'dealing' with her, when the idiot you sent couldn't keep her in hand? How very magnanimous of you."

There was a lengthy silence as David and Kent glared at each other. Kent looked away first and huffed out a breath. Chelsea again felt the tension seep out of the room. Her instincts told her they were through the worst of it now. They'd reacted to the betrayal earlier in the morning, walked the fine line for the power play about being kept out of the loop. Now Kent had aired his annoyance about them — or more properly David — not doing anything about Jennifer having accidently witnessed his actions.

"I've found not being proactive bites you on the arse in the long run," Kent said grudgingly. It sounded more of a parting shot than an opening volley to a new argument.

David nodded, cool and calm once again, his voice sounding at a low tone. "Then it will be my arse, not yours."

There was silence again, but this time it was far less tense, a more normal quiet as they all adjusted their composure.

"So," Chelsea spoke again as the moment drew out, "are we going to make a plan for tonight? Or would you prefer to take some more pot shots at David and me?"

"Let's get to business," Luke said. They all stood once again and crowded around the tables as Kent cleared his throat and gathered some of the blueprints together.

Chapter Three

The crew had gone over the specs until Thaddeus had appeared to decide he'd had enough. He pushed away from the trestle tables with such force that it rattled the thin plywood, then he stood up and glared at the group of them, daring them to object.

"I've had it. We've gone over this to death. We all know what we're doing. We'll know in four hours whether it was good enough. I'm going to the pub."

"We could all use a bit of downtime," Kent agreed with a glance at his watch. "We rendezvous in three hours, at the stationing point. No one be late — or drunk — or else. We'll do our final checks then, before we commit. Any last questions?"

Chelsea looked around the gathered crew, a faint hum of anticipation singing in her veins. They were really going to do this. She felt excited. The nerves would come later.

"Okay then, let's go." Kent dismissed them with a clap of his hands.

Thaddeus was already crossing the large warehouse before Kent had finished speaking. David and Chelsea both stood at a more luxurious pace. Luke remained in his seat, but sketched them a friendly wave goodbye as they gathered their things and left the building.

They didn't speak until David pulled away from the kerb. Only once they were clear did Chelsea speak her thoughts.

"Do you trust Phillipe to honour his word, to bring us to the meeting once we've helped steal the Cézanne?"

"You're thinking if he tested us once he thinks we'll lower our guard now?"

"Wouldn't be the first time one member of a crew killed everyone else to get the glory and money for himself," she pointed out in what she hoped was a reasonable — and not paranoid — manner.

David seemed to think about this for a time.

"My thoughts are that we need to take the gamble anyway," he finally said. "We've come this far — we're so close to finally working out who the head of this smuggling ring is. I'd hate to give up now we're nearly finished."

Chelsea nodded, understanding.

"We'll watch each other's back," she said, "so Kent won't get the drop on us. Where are we headed?"

"Anywhere you like," David said with that glorious lilt to his tone. Chelsea caught his gaze and grinned. Heat shot through her belly. His dark eyes roamed over her, making her flush like a novice.

"Don't crash the car," she murmured, her tone husky with her growing need. "I'd never forgive you if you didn't pay up what you've been promising. My place is closer. If you don't need to pick anything up let's go there."

"Your place it is," he replied. The sensual note of promise in his voice had her shifting in her seat, her knickers now uncomfortably tight and damp.

David changed gears as they gathered speed, and as he worked the shift, his hand grazed her upper thigh. Chelsea barely caught herself before she gasped. Lust, hot and potent, tingled up her thigh and hummed over her clit. She shifted her legs restlessly while staring out of the windscreen.

When David turned the corner—shifting down a gear—and grazed her again, she knew it wasn't accidental.

"You're playing with fire," she warned him.

"You should know by now, the danger is all a part of the thrill for me."

"You have a point." Chelsea chuckled. "But I'm not sure if I can be casual with you. I…trust you too much for that."

David turned his head, caught her eyes with his steady, dark gaze.

"The way I feel about you is anything but casual."

"Well then"—she settled back into her seat—"I can't argue with that."

Having stated her feelings as clearly as she dared for now, Chelsea was willing to leave it. Despite the fact that she'd confessed to loving him, heartfelt statements and the usual female over-analysing of every word, expression and gesture weren't her usual style.

One thing she'd learnt from this work was that she could plot, plan and strategise until kingdom come, but that life—or the universe, whatever—had a tendency to do what it would. Some things you simply couldn't control. Relationships—whether they were sexual liaisons, flings or deeper, more emotional connections—seemed to always fall into that category, she'd found.

From the moment she'd truly begun to trust David she'd slowly found herself falling deeper and deeper in love with him. There was no one she relied on more, or wanted to be closer to. Pushing him into discussing his feelings, or his intentions, or where he saw the two of them moving on to from here would solve nothing—indeed it usually made things far more complicated than they really needed to be.

He'd confessed that this wasn't casual for him, not a quick fling or a 'before we go on the mission' fuck from anyone willing.

For now, that was enough for her.

David pressed the accelerator and zipped through an orange light. Chelsea threw a glance in his direction, struggling to stifle the grin that wanted to break across her face. She reached a hand over and rested it on his upper thigh, cupping his lithe muscle through the warmth of his black denim jeans.

It looked like she wasn't the only one eager to discover the sensual joys that waited around the corner for them both, considering the enormous, thick shaft pressing along the line of his trousers.

Chelsea gave in and grinned. David turned a corner a little too fast, the wheels screeching on the road. He cast her a speaking look and shook his head.

Neither of them said a word. It wasn't really necessary.

* * * *

"Would you like a—umph"—Chelsea dropped her keys and satchel to the floor as David captured her face in his palms, kicked the door closed behind him and kissed her wildly. Her mind blanked, offers of tea, coffee and biscuits evaporating from the sheer heat of their passion as it exploded between them.

With quick movements she shed her coat and scarf, letting them fall to the floor. Throughout this they left their lips locked together, searching with their tongues for the delicious nectar of one another's mouth. Chelsea lifted one foot at a time to unzip and remove her boots. David kicked off his shoes then he traced his hand all over her body.

"So sweet," he muttered as he lifted his head to trail hot, wet kisses down her neck. He worked his fingers nimbly, undoing her shirt and pulling it down her shoulders, snagging it purposely to restrain her arms for one heady, delicious minute.

"Oh fuck," she moaned, more turned on than she could have previously believed possible. Chelsea had never played with being restrained. She naturally liked being in control—both of herself and any situation she found herself in.

The idea of being completely at David's mercy, of him being able to do anything to her, with her...the thought blew her mind. She trusted him completely. It suddenly shone enticingly in front of her, the idea that one day they could explore that dark alley together—a first for her.

She cracked her eyes open—the weight of her lust having closed them without her being conscious of it—and stared at him.

"I never realised being bound could be so...exciting," she panted.

"Oh darling," he groaned, his tone sweet and thick with his own evident arousal. "The things I can show you, the doors we can open for one another. I feel drunk just at the thought."

Chelsea rolled her shoulders, itching to reach her hands out and trace every inch of his body. Part of her snarled, wanting to go into that darker, erotic area. But for their first time together she craved being equal with him, keeping pace with him inch for inch, lick for lick.

David tugged her shirt down, the cuffs catching on her wrists until he pulled once more. When she was released, a freedom surged through her. It took them mere seconds to strip one another completely naked. Craving him like a drug, Chelsea wrapped her arms around his shoulders, drawing their bodies together. She leaned into him, lifted one leg to wrap around his thigh so she could tilt her pelvis up into his erect cock.

Her wet pussy rode over the soft, warm skin of his shaft. Friction sent small frissons of energy jolting through her body, making her feel as if tiny electric shocks danced over her skin. She could almost taste the growing urgency like a fog in the room. Moving her hands around to cup his arse, she squeezed the muscles and massaged them, tracing her fingers in a random pattern up the curve of his glutes to the hollow of his back. An indentation where his spine ended tempted her to trace farther up the long length of his spine.

David inserted one thick leg between her legs, and she rode him in earnest. The change in angle had her clit pressed against his skin, the thin, short hairs of his upper thigh stimulating her. Groaning, distracted, she pressed her pelvis down, grinding her nub against his flesh.

"I can feel your wetness and heat," he moaned.

"I need you," she panted, her head spinning—probably owing to lack of oxygen. Who could breathe when one's body was focused completely on feeling such pleasure?

David nudged her back. He guided her body with his hands on her hips until she moved farther into the main living area and out of the entrance way. Thick carpet covered the floor. A few comfortable chairs, a short coffee table and two couches formed an L shape. David flicked his eyes around the room, even in the heat of passion surveying the area like the pro she knew him to be.

He knelt, tugging her down with him. With a gentle push he urged her onto her back. The carpet felt soft and deep. She loved walking around barefoot and had spent a bloody fortune on the most decadent, luxurious and comfortable blend she could find. Chelsea had always thought the investment a good one—now she resolved never to doubt that judgement again. It was hands down the best money she'd ever spent.

"Remember the second meeting we ever had with the crew? That tiny leather skirt you wore? With the garter belt and tiny red G-string?"

Chelsea choked, caught somewhere between embarrassment and outrage.

"How the hell did you know about the red G-string?"

"We still didn't trust Phillipe, Thaddeus or Luke as far as we could throw them—actually, I still don't— but back then we had agreed to always cover as much of the room between the two of us. I sat opposite you in that meeting, so between us we could have overpowered the other men had it come to that."

"Okay," she replied, her sex-addled brain still not seeing where he was going with this. "I remember. What about it?"

"Whenever you got annoyed and tried to swallow it, forcing yourself to not snap their heads off, you uncrossed then re-crossed your legs," he continued with patience, peppering kisses along the column of her throat, leaving a wet trail that started to curve across her breast. "None of the others were at the correct angle to see more than these luscious, supple thighs of yours. I, however, was privy to tantalising glimpses of that thong and the treasure of your pussy. I've wanted to see it, taste it, explore it ever since that night."

"Oh," she gasped, unable to articulate further as David sucked one hard nipple into his hot mouth. Drawing on it, he created a spark of sensation that raced from her nub, down her breast and ran through her belly finishing at a tingle in her clit.

Her back arched up from the floor. The action was driven by need and not conscious thought. She reached her hands out to thread through David's hair, pleased to find it every bit as silky and soft as it appeared. It fell like gossamer over her skin as she urged him lower.

He didn't need her to guide him at all. Kissing her over and over, he laved her skin with his tongue. The damp spots cooled in the air and added to the growing knot of pleasure lodged deep in her belly. Taking his time, he tasted her at his leisure— mumbling and groaning his appreciation as he made his way over her flat belly, licking and kissing her lower and lower as he made a beeline to her pussy.

When he thrust his tongue into the dent of her belly button, Chelsea moaned as electric pleasure zinged through her. She'd never realised so much of her body was connected—usually sex was much faster and less emotional. David seemed to enjoy her reaction to this and he again fucked her navel with his tongue. Chelsea lifted her body up, twining her fingers again in the strands of his hair to draw him closer.

"Oh, that's...odd, but so fucking good, damn..." Not making sense even to her own ears, Chelsea had no idea how David was supposed to understand her. He seemed caught up in the same insanity, however, for he rumbled a husky laugh, moving his hands lower to stroke at the outer lips of her labia.

"Fuck you're so wet, so ready for me. Tell me this is what you want, what you need, darling."

"Oh yes, please, please. I'm more than ready, David. Please."

"Wonderful," he panted and moved his head lower. Chelsea lifted her head to watch him. One powerful hand rested on her upper thigh, urging her to open for him. She damn well should have known where this was leading, but still she'd been expecting him to fuck her—not scoot down farther, lifting his head so he could watch her being captured, entranced as he ate her.

Dark, black eyes remained steady on her as he delicately, purposefully flicked his tongue out and took a long, slow swipe along the slit of her pussy. Slick juices gleamed over his lips and he swallowed her hungrily. He licked his mouth as if she were a delicacy and quickly returned for seconds.

She widened her eyes, caught between wanting to close them to savour the sensations or capture this moment and burn it on her brain forever. Her mouth fell open, but no sound emerged. Chelsea half thought her brain had imploded, or fried. Whatever had happened, rational thought had fled for the hills.

In some ways she didn't think she'd ever be able to think, or act the same ever again. David was like some catalyst, changing and mutating who and what she was.

They stared at each other as he lapped at her with his tongue, over and over again. He drank from her, clearly enjoying every taste he received. Soon his lips and chin shone wetly, but still he continued. Her breaths came so much faster now, harsher as her lungs struggled to keep up with the rampant thumping of her heart.

The act itself of him eating her out was intensely personal and highly erotic, but watching him and the way his eyes never wavered from her made the whole experience even more stimulating. The thought crossed her mind that he was binding them together, with ropes far stronger than anything physical. By sharing such an insanely intimate act, by having even just this one piece of mutual history, it was something that could never be taken away, never denied, or forgotten, something that even a hundred years from now she'd recall vividly. His every action was branded upon her soul — and his.

Nothing and no one could take this from either of them.

Then he inserted three fingers deep into her pussy. His thick digits stretched her, filled her as much as a regular-sized cock would. Her body accommodated him, but she felt that faint, full burn of possession. Chelsea arched her spine, her head falling gently down. Her curls brushed down her back and stimulated her already over-sensitised flesh.

She cried out, a pleasure-filled sound that could not possibly be mistaken for anything else.

"That's it," David crooned to her. "Scream for me. Cry out loud as you can. I want it all, Chelsea. I want you to lose control, to give everything to me. Everything."

Her inherent stubbornness kicked in. She chuckled, her teasing nature rising to meet his masculine challenge.

"Make me, David," she purred. She lifted her head and caught his gaze again. She could feel the flush of desire on her cheeks and her chest. With her legs splayed wantonly open and his digits inside her pussy she knew the scene had to look erotic. It certainly stimulated her to see him between her legs, his face wet with her juices, his eyes practically black with lust and need.

"If you give me everything I'll return that and more to you," she promised him. "But as always, this is a meeting of equals. I want everything from you too, darling."

He thrust his fingers deeply inside her, curved up to caress over her G-spot. At her words he fucked her harder, faster. Her skin tingled. She felt faintly surprised she didn't shake with the growing arousal as it built steadily within her.

"I'll give you everything," he vowed. The deepness of his tone, the clear meaning was a weight behind every word. All too soon she could feel the climax build. Reaching down to grasp David's shoulders, she urged him up. He lifted himself onto one elbow and crawled up her body, his hand remaining lodged deep inside her.

Digging her nails lightly into the skin of his collarbone, she then tilted her face down so she could hungrily kiss him. She tasted faint, salty muskiness on his lips — her own essence. Far from being repulsed, she enjoyed the way it mingled with his own taste, inside his mouth. Flicking her tongue out, she lapped at him. He seemed faintly surprised, but far from upset. He rumbled a happy sound, somewhere between a murmur and low groan.

"Fuck me," she panted. "I want to feel you stretching me, filling me up."

"Let me get a condom," he groaned and started to pull away. She clung to him.

They'd been working in close proximity for eighteen months. She and David had been bantering, flirting heavily and intimate in all but physical deed particularly for the last six. Agency regulations stipulated all employees have regular, quarterly health checks.

"I'm healthy, and on the pill," she said in a low, soft tone. Chelsea held his gaze, letting him make his own decision.

For her part she knew he'd never hurt her. He held her heart in his hands.

"Are you sure?" he checked as he removed his fingers. She smiled, nodded.

"I'm clean," he continued. "I haven't been...sexually active since my last test. I'm positive I can't cause you harm."

"Then fuck me blind," she purred and pulled him closer.

She could tell she'd taken him by surprise—not by her dirty words, though. Those, she felt sure, were what had caused the twinkle in his eyes. No, he seemed more taken aback that in this day and age she'd willingly offer such a commitment and level of trust.

Eagerly he lodged the large, warm tip of his cock head at her entrance. He waited, seeming to want something. Chelsea stared into his eyes.

"David," she pleaded.

With a groan he pressed inside her, hard.

She'd thought his digits had stretched her. His shaft was far thicker and longer. He seemed to move deeper inside her, until she almost couldn't believe there was still room for him to go. Finally he stopped, his balls snugly cupped against her skin. She gasped and he panted. They were frozen, melded to each other, eyes and bodies locked as intimately as man and woman could be.

The moment stretched out, another one of those bonds tying them together — irrefutable and undeniable — until their dying day. She had never loved a man more, as completely as she did this one currently buried balls-deep inside her. Chelsea honestly couldn't imagine possibly loving a man as much as this, let alone more.

David was her last stop, the man who would forever hold her heart.

The simple but mind-blowing thought had her heart pumping faster. She contracted her pussy around him, squeezing for all she could. He groaned, clearly feeling her inner caress.

"Move in me," she pleaded. "Fuck me, or I might lose my mind."

Words seemed to escape him, so he held her hips and delicately withdrew with infinite slowness. The loss was devastating. For one wild, terrifying moment she felt as if, when David had withdrawn his cock, he had literally taken something hidden from inside her. It was as if he'd removed something of her essential self that she couldn't articulate. He paused as the tip of his head barely touched her outer lips.

He slid back inside her in one smooth, slick, wet motion. David fully and completely lodged himself in her channel once again.

"Oh fuck," she panted, unable to say anything more.

His grip tightened on her waist. Chelsea lifted her hips, wrapped her legs tightly around his waist and locked her ankles together. She reached around his back and grabbed hold of his slick muscles. Holding on for dear life, she lifted up so there was no room to spare between them.

The harsh sound of their heavy breathing filled the room as he pumped faster inside her. Her skin grew damp with sweat, heat infusing her every inch. She felt as if she were burning from the inside, but this was one fire she never wanted to quench.

Over and over he penetrated her, possessing her body and soul.

The knot in her stomach tightened, blossoming out until every part of her felt rigid, waiting for that one thing to knock her over into the broken bliss of orgasm.

David reached one hand between their straining bodies. His eyes never wavered from her—indeed she felt certain he watched her to memorise every twitch, every groan and every sigh so he could remember it always.

They gazed at each other as he sought her clit out with those wicked, nimble fingers. Moving the tender skin of her hood back, he stroked the tip of his finger over her, gently at first, then with a harder, circular motion.

The extra stimulation ignited deep inside her. With a jerking, shuddering quiver her world exploded.

As she screamed her release, her pussy clamped tightly around his thick cock, clenching around him as she shuddered in orgasm. The milking sensation seemed all he needed—or maybe he simply had the control to hold out long enough to let her come first and he could finally relax his own tenuous grip on his climax. Either way, David shattered. Pumping within her furiously hard he rode out his own orgasm.

Thick, hot fluid gushed from his tip, filling her with the wet essence. Chelsea had never had unprotected sex before and marvelled at the difference. Seed leaked out of her opening as she overflowed, small amounts trickling down her thigh. She didn't mind. It merely added to the intimacy of the moment, that her body literally brimmed with his fluid.

They remained locked tightly together, devouring each other silently with hungry eyes. They both panted to catch their breaths. Those few moments immediately after such an intense, magical moment were the most sensual, intimate she'd ever experienced. A part of her felt she had truly bared her soul to David, and he his to her. She read love, vulnerability, worry and pride in his gaze.

She smiled at him, hoping that her own love for him showed through just as clearly.

The sweat beading her skin began to cool in the chilly winter air. She shivered, and immediately the gentlemanly nature in David—never very far from the fore in him—reared its head.

"Let's get you to bed," he said.

She chuckled. "I thought we'd just finished doing that," she teased him as he withdrew from her pussy. He laughed, cupped her face and kissed her tenderly.

Chelsea lapped up everything he gave her. His heart and soul seemed to be in the kiss. Gentleness, warmth and passion infused the sensual caress, making it different from any other encounter she'd had. Just as lovingly, she returned it.

"We never made it as far as the bed," he reminded her as he pulled back. "Maybe this time we'll be luckier."

Chelsea let him help her to her feet, surprised that her legs were faintly wobbly. This was certainly a day of firsts—no man, ever, had made her legs tremble.

"I'm not sure my heart could handle getting luckier," she replied, more than half serious. "It nearly imploded from our actions on the floor. Imagine what a real bed could do."

David glanced at the spot on the carpet, still holding the faint indentation of where his body had pressed her into the woven threads.

"I've thought about doing something similar to that in practically every conceivable place and position," he said seriously. "I'm sure your heart can stand a repeat performance in bed."

She chuckled and took his hand in hers, threading their fingers intimately together.

"Maybe," she conceded. "I'll grab a quick shower, then maybe you can show me some of these other positions you've fantasised about. If they're anything like what that just felt like I'm sure I'll be amenable to any number of your suggestions."

His look was so hot, so steeped with naked, hungry arousal that it took her breath away.

"I'm sure I have more than a few ideas you might enjoy."

She shivered, partly from the cool air but also from the intensity of his desire. She loved him, craved him, needed him—but he wanted her with an almost feral need. It thrilled her, excited her, but also frightened her a little. She'd never come across such a soul-deep yearning.

"Come on," he said softly, tugging her deeper into her flat. "You wanted a shower. I'll try to restrain myself."

Chelsea tugged back on his hand when he started to step forward. Lifting her free hand she cupped his face, drew him to her and kissed him with every ounce of need and hunger within her, loosening her hold of her control for a wild, freeing moment. When she pulled back they both panted once again.

"Don't ever restrain yourself for me," she insisted. "I cherish the person you are, exactly as you truly are. We've seen too much, been through too much together to pretend. Especially now. So don't. Okay?"

He nodded, answering her silently while seeming to chew over her words. She kissed him again, tenderly this time until they both parted.

"Let me show you the bedroom," she said. "You can keep the bed warm while I wash up. I'll only be a few minutes."

"I think I can wait that long," he promised as she led him down the hall.

Grinning, she opened the door and went through. She let go of his hand as she continued through the room towards the en suite where a small bathroom lay.

"Really? I'm not sure I can," she teased. Blowing him a kiss she moved into the bathroom and turned on the taps, unable to hear over the water any reply he might have made.

Chapter Four

The shower had been running for about five minutes. David had cleaned himself quickly at the basin and had gone back into Chelsea's bedroom. The room reminded him strongly of her. He half believed that had he broken in, he could have guessed it was hers.

An enormous bed took up much of the space, neatly made with a duvet of mingled blues and greens and matching pillow cases. Elegantly framed landscapes she'd evidently brought with her from her home in Dublin showed lush green hills that seemed to go on forever. The paintings, along with the bed, spoke longingly of endless walks getting lost in those wilds of Ireland.

He could so easily imagine himself, hand in hand with his love, discovering adventures and intimacy in those boundless fields of a million shades of green. David stared at the images for minutes, his desire for this amazing woman growing as he heard her moving in the shower. She hummed a light, happy tune. The sound of water sloshing over her skin came to him her hands sluicing the perfumed soap from her body onto the tiled shower base.

Steam rolled out of the open door and the faint scent of wild flowers reached his senses.

'Don't ever restrain yourself for me... I cherish the person you are... I'm not sure I can wait that long...'

Chelsea's words from earlier echoed in his head. His mind still tried to come to grips with the nature of what she'd shown him minutes ago. David had always known he was a deep man. On the surface he was not complicated at all—at least not to the casual observer.

A quiet man, intelligent and loyal, before going undercover he'd never wanted for lovers—women willing to connect with him for a romantic interlude. Working with the Agency, however, meant keeping not only odd hours, but secrets, too. Women, he'd quickly learnt, were not fans of secrets, especially when they encompassed an enormous section of one's life.

Why was he cancelling dinner again? He was late to the movies, party or rendezvous, why? Even such simple enquiries as 'How was your day?' could only be answered in vague terms so many times before frustration set in for his companions.

The few people who had managed to scratch his surface had discovered that, like most people, he actually was incredibly complicated. David would never consider quitting his work. It fulfilled the need inside him to balance the scales, to right wrongs and try to protect his country and the way of life he felt they were all entitled to.

Just because someone was strong and craved power did not mean that they had to crush those beneath and around them. That was something he'd believed in from childhood, standing up to bullies, protecting those he cared about, doing something rather than just sitting back bitching and complaining.

'David is an intelligent, caring boy, but has a temper and can't control his impulses when a friend/fellow student is being picked on...' was written in various forms on many of his school report cards.

Since his parents and siblings had never been fussed about it—his father and uncles even teaching him how to fist fight properly and instilling strict principles and honour in him—he'd never given his instincts much of a second thought. Certainly he'd never paid attention to people who'd insisted there were 'gentler' or nicer ways to deal with such bullies.

Talking was all well and good, but it didn't help when one's opponent was effectively a brick wall, refusing to listen or carry out a dialogue.

David strongly believed in manners, in being courteous, and he got a warm glow each time Chelsea thanked him for opening a door or acting in a courtly manner. She had understood from the start that it was an inherent part of him and had never tried to insist that she do such things herself in his presence.

She was such an independent, strong-willed woman that he'd privately been surprised but pleased. Then again, she, too, was an intricate, complex female. As so frequently happened, his thoughts turned back to the seductress in the bathroom.

She seemed to genuinely want him, lust for him, even love him. The knowledge thrilled him. He'd loved her for months, soaking up her every smile, every glance she threw at him whether she was laughing or chiding or simply debating and questioning their work. He loved the way her dark blue eyes shone with intelligent curiosity.

He adored her. More than that, he treasured her. He knew he would protect her above any other living person. Her safety and happiness came first with him. He couldn't deny it or pretend to feel differently.

'...*maybe you can show me some of these other positions you've fantasised about... I'm sure I'll be amenable...*'

Lust surged through him. The heat of his need angled sharply down his body, filling his cock with blood. The quickness and force of his arousal washed over him almost painfully. His dick swelled with it, jutting up and demanding attention. For all of a minute he wrestled with himself, convinced he needed to give her time and space.

David chuckled and shook his head.

Chelsea was not some delicate little flower needing time to come to terms with the new intimacy created within their relationship. Even now she was washing his seed from her legs, from her pussy. Recalling again her faith and trust in him, her willingness to be as deeply intimate as two people could possibly be, had his body shaking with the urge to take her over and over again.

He couldn't possibly wait another moment, courtesy be damned.

David climbed off the bed and stalked across the room. He entered the bathroom. Chelsea was rinsing her body. He watched the blurred outline of her sensual frame like a voyeur through the frosted glass of the shower. Moving to the door he saw her face lift as she caught sight of him.

"I'm just getting out now," she said.

David opened the cubicle, the catch making a snick sound. The steam billowed out and warmed him. He cast his eyes lovingly down her slick, naked form. Covered in water, glistening, she was a highly erotic vision. For a second he was at a loss for words. Their gazes met and he felt trapped, ensnared. He never wanted to look away from those perfect eyes. "I think you need help soaping yourself," he said, surprised by the thickness in his tone. Need clamoured at him, pushing every other thought out of his mind.

She grinned as she stepped back, inviting him to share the small cubicle with her. "I'm positive you need help getting clean too," she purred.

He loved the way sinful sex rolled from her in waves. She tempted him on every level. For a second he imagined thrusting his hard, hot cock deeply into those lush lips, watching their pouting fullness close around his shaft and suck the ever-loving hell from him.

He nearly groaned at the vision. She seemed to read him easily—though his thoughts couldn't have been too hidden considering his erect dick bounced against the flat plane of his belly.

Chelsea reached out to touch him first, her hand slender, warm and wet. With her other hand she grabbed a small bottle of shower gel, squirted some and spread it over his chest.

They were silent as they caressed each other, passing the bottle back and forth as they soaped one another. He loved the softness of her skin. She felt so delicate to him, so breakable. It was an odd feeling, for he knew Chelsea so well.

She was strong, fierce, like a womanly warrior from ancient times. Seeing her like this—vulnerable, naked, feminine—was almost as intimate as watching her face change as he'd thrust his cock into her willing body. They had shared parts of themselves he knew would bind them together forever, no matter how this turned out. That thought made him hot as hell.

"I want to do things to you," he confessed in the sensual moment that blossomed as they washed each other. "I keep imagining what you'll look like with me in your mouth. How bliss and need transformed your face when I penetrated you. I'm not sure I can ever get enough of you."

She rinsed the soap from him, gliding her hands over his chest, his stomach and arms. David angled Chelsea so she stood beneath the spray and he could rinse her as well. When they were done she pressed her breasts into his chest, threading their legs intimately together. She lifted her face and kissed the edge of his jaw.

"I want that too," she replied in a low tone. "Even though I'm satisfied, can feel the passionate exhaustion in my bones, I crave you. I want to do everything with you, play out all of our fantasies. I'm just as addicted as you, David."

Satisfaction washed over him. They were definitely on the same page. He moved his hands down the curve of her back, water sluicing as he touched her. He cupped his palms around her arse, enjoying the soft, firm roundness of them. He drew her closer. Chelsea's eyes widened and his masculine instinct quivered. He'd come close to touching a nerve, or perhaps one of those fantasies they'd discussed.

Slowly, carefully, respectful of the fact that he might be misreading her, David held each of the globes of her pert, round arse. Moving the cheeks apart just a little, he gazed steadily at her, waiting for Chelsea to move or deny him, to draw a line. She did neither. Indeed her pupils dilated with lust, the colour seeming to darken into an almost violet blue shade.

"Oh, darling," he purred, lust now riding him hard. Stretching his index finger out, he slowly trailed the tip between her cheeks and made a slow line for the tiny, tightly puckered hole of her anus. When he stroked over her furled skin, she moaned, arched her body into his, simultaneously pressing her breasts into him and tilting her hips to press her arse back into his caress.

Breath escaped him. Need slammed into him.

Chelsea wriggled her arse, urging him on.

Panting with need now, he joined a second digit in with the first and he explored the tender flesh, seeking nerves that would increase the pleasure. He knew this part of her, the thin, delicate membrane, would be incredibly sensitised to his every caress. Chelsea threw her head back decadently and moaned, clearly conveying her pleasure at his touch.

"Is this one of those secret fantasies?" he asked.

Even to his own ears the tone sounded darkly dangerous. Hunger hammered at him, and the elemental, animalistic side to him wanted nothing as much as to bend her over right there in the shower, spread her cheeks wide and plunge into her, to claim her arse as he had claimed her pussy—to own her body and soul as she did him. Chelsea might not know or understand it yet, but she held his heart, his lust and his spirit, everything he was. The desire for that to be reciprocated was a fire burning within him.

She sensually wrapped a wet, slender arm around his neck. Chelsea looked into his eyes, her gaze as stormy, deep and unfathomable as the sea.

"I've fantasised about anal play, anal possession, yes," she confessed. "But...but well...it's never come together for me. The right man, the right time... It never all lined up."

Deep in his soul a beast howled, denied. David moved his fingers, though remained caressing her arse. It took him a moment to struggle with himself, but he held onto his control, his restraint, and eased himself mentally back from that dark, intoxicating desire. They had forever, he reminded himself. There was no need to try everything in their first true day together.

"I understand," he replied, strain in his tone.

Chelsea shook her head.

"I'm not being clear," she said. "I was trying to be delicate, but I should have known better—I'm not like that, I'm more forward and blunt usually. David, I'd love to explore anal sex with you, but I've never done it before so...so we can't just jump in. I'll need...preparation. I want to do this with you, but you'll be my first."

Not for the first time around this beautiful woman, words failed him. A darkness he didn't often acknowledge inside himself blossomed, grinned feral and smug inside the depths of his chest. Unable to explain what her trust and faith meant to him, David instead lifted a hand to tilt her chin.

Lowering his head, he then slowly pressed their lips together and kissed her with all the passion, love, need and gratefulness that swirled around in him. She returned his kiss just as hard and hungry. Love and excitement burst between them. Chelsea met him press for press, her passion as ardent as his. She parried her tongue with his, her need clearly equal to own yearning. She was his equal, his partner, his soul mate in every respect.

Slowly they pulled apart. David felt drunk on their passion, on the excitement of knowing what was to come. He was her first. She was giving herself to him, a part she had never shared with anyone else. The barbarian he kept locked away wanted to pound his chest and crow with delight.

He stared at her, drinking in and memorising the sight of her. Every detail of her face, her smile, the way her eyes crinkled when she grinned at him in that naughty manner, he burned it all on his brain, etched it into his deepest soul.

"Let's go," he whispered.

Chelsea reached out and turned off the taps. David opened the cubicle door, stepped out and got them both towels. He dried himself in record time. Wanting to give Chelsea a moment alone in case she needed it, he pressed a lingering kiss to her lips, her body warm and literally steaming in the cool air.

"We'll take our time," he promised her after lifting his head away. "There's no rush, we have forever."

"I know," she replied with that naughty grin. "I'll just be a minute."

David lifted his hand to lightly caress her face. He loved her with everything inside him, adored her more than mere words could ever convey. Hanging up the towel he cast a final glance at her before leaving the bathroom.

Chelsea had learnt at a young age to never show fear. In her book, the moment you let people know you were afraid it was all over. It was part of the reason she always showed such bravado, regardless of the situation or her true feelings.

She didn't fear David, not for one instant.

The man could be dangerous, deadly even. He could be merciless and devious. Those were aspects of him she admired and could even be grateful for. It was also much of what those who glimpsed only at his surface saw. The Agent. The patriot, deeply loyal and unwavering in his dedication to getting an often hard, dirty, thankless job done properly.

Beneath that, however, was the complicated, intricate, endlessly fascinating man she had come to know, respect and love beyond all reason. He was kind, compassionate and acted with a ceaseless, genuinely chivalrous manner.

She knew without a doubt he craved to fuck her up the arse, to pound into her and possess her every most intimate secret. The thickness of his cock in the shower moments earlier as he'd stroked her private passage had been proof positive of that. But the second—the very moment—he'd thought she was not amenable to the suggestion he had backed off. Not tried to wheedle or convince her, talk her into it or explain how wonderful it could be. He'd stepped back and had respected her—her decisions and beliefs—without question.

Had she not been in love with him already, adored him more than the stars and sun and moon, she would have fallen a little for him in that moment.

Dry, Chelsea hung up her towel and stole a glance at her reflection in the mirror.

Just minutes ago she'd pleaded with him to have sex with her—unprotected. Part of her felt there could be no greater trust, no more intimate sharing between two people. Now she wasn't so sure. Chelsea half expected to see something different about her face, but there was nothing. No literal bonds tied them together, no stamp on her forehead or neck stating 'Property of David Greer'.

She could feel them becoming more entwined, the need and power between them growing and hardening. Soon it would be impossible to contemplate anything without him by her side. She huffed out a tiny laugh. Who the hell was she kidding? Right now she couldn't imagine life without him. She wanted him by her side, needed him in her life.

Who the hell was she and what had she done with Chelsea Atchison?

Grinning at her reflection, the moment she had asked the question she knew the answer. Chelsea Atchison was a hard-core, never-say-die, stubborn-arsed secret agent. She wasn't afraid of anything, not even of being tied body and soul to a man who could destroy her with ease, should he choose to do so.

She blew a kiss to her reflection.

Trust like this, soul deep and terrible in its intensity, ran both ways. She'd no more turn her back on David, or harm him, than she'd shave her head bald and sever a limb. Deep in her heart, she knew he felt the same about her.

Turning on her heel, she then headed into the bedroom. David had pulled the covers back on her bed, a tube of lubricant he'd evidently found in the top drawer of her bedside table on the mattress next to him. Unsure what to say—was there even a protocol for this?—she was relieved when he simply and silently held his hand out to her.

Relief washed through her and she crossed to the bed with an eagerness she hadn't felt since her first few sexual encounters. She climbed up next to him, wrapped her arms around his broad shoulders and kissed his lips hungrily. It didn't seem to matter how often they did this, their kisses never got old, never lost the intensity of that first one. Desire burned through her, the dark desire to give up all control, to lose herself in his heated embrace and forget the rest of the world even existed. Who cared about smuggling rings, terrorists or threats to national security when David cradled her in his arms, when his kiss could set fire to her every nerve and when with one hot glance from him she wanted to shed her knickers, spread her legs and feel his cock penetrate her every orifice.

Her every orifice.

Chelsea could kiss David until the world ended, the sun imploded and all the angels and demons of the universe came trumpeting in. Even then, she could imagine herself begging for one more kiss, one more caress, just a little more and then she'd deal with it all. Her body flushed, every inch of her aware of this man who held her soul. Juices dripped down her thigh, her passion heightened by the knowledge of what they were going to share.

David nudged her onto her knees.

"Play with your nipples," he commanded.

Groaning, not one to usually follow any order, Chelsea found herself eagerly complying. She knew the exact pressure that would send her to the stars, the right twists and manner that she loved. Turning her head as she stimulated herself, she saw David behind her, studying her intently. She knew him well enough by now to know that he drank in everything, and would file this knowledge away for intimate use later.

That thought made her hotter.

"It's going to burn," he whispered darkly to her. Chelsea heard the cap of the lube pop open and felt her heart hammer at the knowledge of what was coming. He touched the round globes of her arse with cool, moist fingers. He spread her cheeks apart with his gentle hands and pressed his slick digits against her anal passage.

"You've been trained to shut pain out—I know this for I've been through the same. But don't compartmentalise it, trust me on this. I don't know how to express it better, but embrace it, lean into it. When you first started endurance training, once you mentally talked through that first burn of pain, where you wanted to give up and stop—well, you know how it is. If you keep going, the pain goes away, and the adrenaline kicks in, the pleasure starts. This is the same."

As he spoke he traced his finger teasingly around the tiny entrance. She felt the breach of just the tiniest tip. He slicked more lube inside her, easing his passage. Then he was gone, more gel squirted and he was back.

Chelsea turned to watch him, still toying with her nipples, her breaths coming hard and fast as her pleasure spiked. She understood what David had told her, and part of her marvelled that, even lost to his lust as he so clearly was, he still thought of her enjoyment, still wanted her to be with him, matching him step for step and thrust for thrust.

She'd seen him fatally wound a man in the past—someone who had threatened to blow their covers and expose them to certain death. David had shown little care or remorse, killing the man and cleaning up the mess. He'd been surprised when she'd offered to help him remove the evidence, but he'd accepted with a nod, simply not concerned by the darkness of death and destruction.

That was the only side to him almost anyone knew. She saw so much more, and their new intimacies had only deepened that knowledge.

Slowly, with copious amounts of lube, David finally eased a finger inside her anal passage. Chelsea moved one of her hands down to stimulate her clit, her pleasure heightening. As he had described, the penetration of that single digit burned, but it was a darkly intense, pleasure-filled ache. She felt full, stretched and skewered. But at the same time a million nerves were being stimulated, sending shocks of pleasure coursing across her body.

The dichotomy of the situation took her breath away. Yes, it was painful, but it was also the headiest bliss, the darkest, most sensual experience she'd ever had.

"More," she pleaded.

Proving he trusted her fully, David took her at her word. Slowly, he inserted a second finger into her arse. She cried out, the discomfort of being stretched hard now blurred with the pleasure. Overwhelmed, Chelsea didn't know whether to rock her hips back and plunge his digits their full depth inside her or pull away and end the torment.

Recalling his description, she understood what he'd meant now. Embracing the pain, she breathed deeply, sucking air into the fullness of her lungs and adding more oxygen into her blood — just as she did when the first wave of tiredness came over her as she ran.

Pushing mentally through the barrier, she opened herself to the new sensations bombarding her, rolled the glut of feelings up until she focused on the pleasure and moved past the agony of this new possession.

Wave after wave of intoxicating sensations rocked through her. David began thrusting inside her tight, virginal channel, fucking her slowly, lazily almost. Her need ratcheted up, hunger burning through her from within.

She thrust her hips back, leaning her chest towards the mattress to shove her arse higher into the air, pushing his fingers deeply into her. By accepting the pain, she craved it more, the darkness overwhelming her.

"More, David, please!" she pleaded.

Answering her without words he fucked into her faster, harder now. He stretched her thin passage, the lubricant easing his way and making wet sucking noises as he moved with speed. Nerves were stimulated, and with her clit receiving attention from her own hand, Chelsea's desire climbed higher, spiking with this new sensation. Tension rocked her body and she knew it wouldn't be long now. The threatening wave of orgasm rumbled on her horizon.

"Fuck me, David," she cried out, losing herself as she felt the storm approaching. Electricity seemed to spark from her body, the intensity of her emotions, the feelings and sensations her lover brought out in her like nothing she'd ever experienced before.

Letting go of her control, she willingly gave herself fully and completely into his care.

"David, please, just fuck me hard, deep in my arse, right now!" she screamed.

"Oh shit, darling, you're going to kill me," he groaned, hunger etched in his tone.

She felt him withdraw and nearly wept with the loss. She heard the liquid sound of more lube being squeezed and seconds later she felt the enormous, hot head of his cock pressed to her arse. Turning her head, she saw fierce concentration reflected on David's face.

Lifting up she looked down and swallowed hard at the picture. His thick, hard shaft looked enormous, swollen fully. His head was mammoth, the glans so much bigger than her puckered entrance. For a second doubt assailed her. Surely he couldn't fit in there? The girth of his tip was nearly double the size of her hole.

Hard, sharp pressure assailed her as he pressed just the first inch into her passage. The lube assisted him, slick and wet, but her breath caught at that first whip of a burn that promptly blossomed into a dark pressure. Stroking her clit, she drew in a deep breath.

David's hands were warm on her hips, his grip tight but not bruising. He exerted a small bit of pressure, urging her to change angles. She complied and it eased some of the pain. When his shaft stroked over a sensitive cluster of nerves, pleasure shot through her, dulling the hurt and shocking her senses.

"Open for me, darling," David panted. "You're so fucking tight, so hot, I've never felt anything like this before."

His words drew her into his spell, a sensually woven latticework that snared her even as she eagerly entered its embrace. Tweaking her nipples with one hand, she slowly stroked her clit with her other fingers. As before, the dichotomy of good and bad blurred, and her enjoyment rose again. This second time, though, it was darker, deeper and far more intense. She could have sworn she heard thunder rumbling in the distance, the building pressure gathering within her promising a climax unlike anything she knew could exist.

David filled her completely, his cock lodged into full penetration. He removed himself and pressed back in, working slowly, the strain visible on his face.

"Let go," she pleaded. "Give yourself totally to me. You can't possibly hurt me, love."

Something in her words seemed to resonate with him, and just as she had submitted to him, fully and willingly, so too did he reciprocate. He threw his head back, shouted out a primitive cry, and lost his control. His moves became harsh, instinctive. Increasing his speed he plunged in and out of her, fucking her arse with wild abandon.

Words couldn't express what it felt like. Intense. Erotic. Darkly delicious. None of the labels even came close.

Overwhelmed, Chelsea's body shook with reaction to the possession and branding he cast upon her. Her response was no less, though decidedly feminine.

She opened herself to him, eagerly followed where he took her. She met him, thrust for thrust, pressing her arse back and accepting him for all he was. Her breath escaped in short pants. Tears sprang to her eyes at the explosive, exhausting level of emotion he wrought from her.

Her eyes fluttered shut. Her orgasm crashed over her, taking her by surprise. It was like being hit by a tidal wave, the force of it damn near painful as it washed over and through her.

She screamed, a fierce sound that shook her to the core.

David was barely a second behind her. His thrusts were hard now, bruisingly so. He plumbed her depths, his limbs shaking as his cock spurted, ejaculating his seed and filling her ravished hole.

He roared, his masculine shout echoing with hers, reverberating around the room until she felt the walls should be shaking from the noise.

Chelsea could feel the warmth seeping out of her arse and down her leg, but she couldn't have cared less. Aftershocks sang through her body, twitching her muscles as exhaustion washed over her. She collapsed forward onto her belly, the mattress taking the brunt of her fall. Still locked inside her, David moved down with her, the warmth of his body protecting her from the chill in the room.

She could smell the pleasant scent of their mingled essences. Salty, musky, floral—they melded together to an indefinable smell she recognised as *them*.

David wrapped his arms around her waist, drawing them together until they spooned on the mattress, her back pressed to his chest, his dick still inside her butt. Chelsea wriggled to fit herself closer to his warm frame, never wanting him to leave her, hoping they could stay like this forever.

Nothing would ever be the same again. She knew it now, embraced it.

David lifted a hand and stroked her hair, the gesture infinitely tender. She smiled.

"I love you," she said softly.

She hoped he wouldn't be surprised or upset at her words. She knew they loved one another, had known it for a while now. Knowing it on an intellectual level, however, was different to expressing the words so finitely aloud. There could be no questions or hesitation, no dissembling from this point in. For, once stated, they couldn't be retracted. More than that, they were so entwined now, their hearts and souls so knitted together, that it would be devastating to her should they split apart.

"I love you too."

He kissed the nape of her neck. She shivered and turned her head to stare at him.

"I love that lilt in your tone you get when you're tender with me," she confessed. "I can hear it sometimes, like a siren call from home. When you said that, those four words, it's like a lure to me, drawing me ever closer to you."

"I'll keep that in mind," he replied with a grin, the tone still present. She chuckled and turned her head back, snuggling into his embrace.

"Be careful you use it for good," she teased. "I'd be tempted to do anything for you when you use that tone. 'Tis a terrible weapon you have there."

Only as the words echoed in the room did she realise the double meaning he could read into it. She laughed, knowing she didn't need to explain or speak further. His dark chuckle proved he knew exactly what she had meant — and unconsciously implied.

Her heart overflowed with love for this complex, marvellous man whom she adored.

Chapter Five

David's world had been completely shattered. He knew now, without any question, that he could not survive without this amazing woman. The way she'd surrendered herself to him, urged him to give the same to her... Words failed him.

They lay cupped together, relaxed and as comfortable as if they'd been lovers for decades. He wanted to close his eyes and ignore the world, shut it out entirely and relish getting to know every inch of Chelsea's skin, in learning what made her sigh and scream, writhe and plead for mercy.

Sadly, his duty weighed on his conscience. They had a job to do. If she decided to step away he would urge her to leave for Dublin the moment she could finish packing, but he could not do so — wouldn't leave his work unfinished, these criminals out to harm other innocent people.

The fact that he felt so strongly this way suggested Chelsea would have a similar if not identical belief. They were both stubborn, wilful people. David knew at times there would be fireworks and arguments where their shouts could make the house around them tremble. But they loved each other with a rare passion he'd never seen in others.

The future looked bright, delicious, enticing.

He glanced at the clock and sighed. He was loath to bring up the fact that they had to be moving, but soon it would be impossible to ignore.

"I know," Chelsea murmured. The laziness in her voice, the sensual undertones, had his cock twitching hungrily. David firmly squashed the small flickers of desire that lapped in the base of his balls.

Now was not the time, tempting as this siren was.

He stroked a hand down the long, dark curls, marvelling again at their silky softness.

"I hate to be the bearer of bad news," he said, leaning on his accent, using that lilt she'd confessed drove her wild. "But we need to get dressed and ready—we have to go rob the National Gallery, darling."

Chelsea laughed. She dipped a shoulder and moved delicately away from him—his cock sliding out of her warm, wet ass—and turned to face him on her bed. When she wrapped an arm around his waist he let her draw him close, snuggling them together.

"If anyone else had said that to me in a moment like this I'd think they were insane. But you somehow make it sound dangerous and completely normal at the same time."

He grinned, bent his head forward and pressed a hot, searching kiss to that lush, red mouth of hers. Her cheeks were flushed delightfully, her lips moist and plump from their earlier passion. Pulling away so he could sit up David took a deep breath. He stared down at the decadent, luscious vision Chelsea made.

Burning the delicious image of her splayed, ravished and passion-spent on the sheets into his brain, he held the picture close to his heart, another treasure to add to the growing number in his soul.

"No other man will ever say such things to you," he vowed, a smile taking the possessiveness from the words. "Besides, I'm sure in time you'll say equally strange things to me. It can be our secret."

Resting a hand on the mattress next to her head, he used it to hold his weight as he bent, kissed her again and ran his free hand through her curls, spreading them over the sheets and mussing them further. Pulling back, he studied her again and smiled tenderly.

"You're the most beautiful, treasured person in my world," he said. Chelsea's dark blue eyes became enormous and her cheeks flushed a deeper red.

Not wanting to ruin the perfection of the moment with talk, he smiled silently, then climbed from the bed and moved to the bathroom. Opening the shower cubicle so he could reach inside, David then leaned in to adjust the water to the heat he liked. Satisfied, he stepped in and quickly washed himself.

Part of his mind—the hidden Neanderthal man who in reality resided in most men to one degree or other—hated removing the evidence of the passion and possession he'd shared with Chelsea. He wanted to wear her scent with pride, know her juices coated his body and that nothing could separate them.

Reality, however, was an ugly bitch. He needed to focus on the task at hand, not have sticky skin and clothes rubbing him wrong. Nor did he need the added distraction of Chelsea's scent on his every inch, as well as standing next to him as they broke into the Gallery.

Clean, he was about to turn off the faucets when Chelsea opened the cubicle door. She grinned at him, a warm, welcoming invitation. His cock stirred.

"No pouncing," she insisted. "We have little enough time as it is."

He nodded, knowing the truth in her words but still unable to squash the desire to take her over and over. She was more addictive than any drug to him.

"I'm done here. Let me go grab our clothes and I'll be dressed and decent when you're finished."

The laughter in her eyes drew him in, promising untold pleasure.

"You might be dressed, but I hope you're never decent around me."

Chuckling, they kissed, a hot, quick press of lips that promised much more.

They swapped positions. David reached for the towel, wondering how the hell he was supposed to focus with this vixen by his side and in his blood. The thought that if he couldn't remain on task they might be separated as working partners acted like a wash of cold water. They were a brilliant team, bloody made for each other. After such a long time undercover they could read nuances in the other's body language better than some twins, and more importantly they understood how each other thought. They were made for work like this, perfectly matched in every way. David refused to let his lack of control threaten that.

He dried himself and returned to the front room to collect their gear. While making his way back to the bedroom he checked out of the windows, one of many security habits he had no intention of repressing. In the bedroom he slowly dressed. As he pulled each item of clothing on, he mentally prepared himself, getting back into the work frame of mind. If he didn't concentrate, pick up every signal, catch every hint of the tableau before them, it could result in their death — or, worse, capture.

David was responsible not just for his safety, but for Chelsea's. That thought acted better than the strongest pep-talk or shackles of responsibility. Nothing would hurt her. Nothing.

A minute later Chelsea stalked out of the bathroom, freshly washed and dried, and clearly with her head back in the game. Warm feelings emanated from her, a caring and love that neither could deny, but her features were set again, her gaze laser sharp and her posture that no longer of a languid lover, but of a working professional.

Chelsea nodded at him, and he tilted his head in acknowledgement.

She crossed to the tall boy, opened drawers and dressed promptly. Black lacy knickers, a matching bra and thin socks. Tight, fitted black jeans and a long-sleeved shirt that clung to her luscious curves. Chelsea opened her wardrobe and pulled out a jacket and laid it on the rumpled bed. She ran a brush through her silky curls, then lifted her hands and started to plait her hair with a speed and efficiency that showed she'd done this a million times.

"Send the signal to McIlroy," she said. "We need him to know this is going down. He'll at least be ready for our call later on. We're still supposed to meet with Phillipe's boss after we steal the Cézanne, aren't we?"

"I believe so, but you know Kent, he's a twitchy bugger after a heist. Still, McIlroy will know we'll contact him as soon as we have data on who Phillipe answers to. Hard to believe we're on the home stretch with this," David mused as he pulled his sleeve up to expose his watch.

A classic man's watch, it had a few buttons and three dials in the face. He pressed a button three times in quick succession. Nothing appeared to happen, though both he and Chelsea knew it had emitted a beacon back to the Dublin office, on a wavelength dedicated to David, Chelsea and this particular mission. There'd be no doubt who'd sent the signal, and would soon follow with a communication.

David took a deep breath, pulled his shirt sleeve back down and looked at his partner. They shared a silent gaze for a few heartbeats, neither needing to wish the other luck or even say a word. It had become their routine to not wish good luck, or any form of verbal assurance before they set out at times like this. They both felt it tempted fate, something neither was keen to do.

Holding out his hand, David waited while Chelsea smiled and took it. They twined their fingers intimately together, a thrill searing his senses as proof he'd not imagined their earlier chemistry, the deep, pleasant ache in his muscles reminding him of their previous shenanigans. They shared a final kiss and were ready to move.

"Almost ready," she murmured huskily as she collected her kit — a small satchel with a large strap that wrapped around her chest. The satchel was of a size to fit two or three hardback books, enough to fit their gear in it, anything they might need to carry, but small enough to rest along the length of her body and not be particularly noticeable.

He wore an identical one, with his gun, spare ammunition, a set of lock picks, a thin coil of rope and a number of other items he considered essential for any job. With their work one could never be quite certain what would be useful and what would not.

David had learnt long ago to err on the side of caution. With a handful of tools and items, he could pretty much make do in nearly any situation.

Tucked into an outside pocket of his bag was a thumb-sized electronic device that looked a bit like a portable MP3 player. It was actually a very powerful voice-activated recorder, which they planned to use along with some discreetly taken pictures to identify the final link in the smuggling chain.

But first they had to steal the Cézanne.

They spent a precious few minutes checking their gear, then they were ready.

"Let's go," Chelsea said. With a nod he followed her back out onto the street.

It was time.

* * * *

"So as best I can figure they've reacted pretty much how we expected," Luke said.

The five of them pored over a single sheet of paper laid out on the table in the booth they occupied. The small pub had three flat-screen TVs on various walls showing three different footy matches. The patrons either watched while they sipped their beers, or a few couples enjoyed a cosy meal together. No one paid the group the least mind.

"I've scouted and timed the rounds and this is what we're facing. The patrols have been tripled — so now instead of one pair there are three. Don't be fooled, though. The extra pairs have been carefully briefed. Whenever a call or alert goes out, one pair remains where they are. The other two pairs split up and go in separate directions to answer and survey the surrounding areas. That's something we hadn't expected," Luke spoke.

"We'd assumed they'd remain together in a giant clump." Thaddeus nodded. "That's smart, whoever instructed the patrols to act like that. So we can't divert attention from the areas we want by setting up a flare, like we'd hoped."

"No, we've had to ditch that idea," Kent agreed. "Instead, what we'll need to do is divide and conquer ourselves. I still think we need a diversion—dealing with a six-man team is too much for us, especially when everyone out there will be trigger happy. We continue with parts of the plan and adapt as the situation calls for it. That's why we always planned to have this meeting to get everything straight."

"Have they increased the frequency of patrols?" Chelsea asked as she bent over the schematic. "This whole section should still be far less active. The amateur award winners from the local Art College, while interesting, have no real monetary value as yet. And this corridor where they're being shown leads directly to the smaller 'Where did they come from?' gallery that we're interested in."

"That's the bad news," Luke added.

Chelsea's heart sank, her spirits with it. Bad news so close to a dangerous run like this never boded well. David sat beside her and moved his hand slightly, his fingers brushing the outer edge of her thigh. The caress was brief and so subtle it could easily have been nothing, but it sent warmth flowing through her.

He must have felt that same twisting sensation in his stomach and wanted to offer her comfort. She let the corner of her mouth twitch in a tiny smile of thanks. She didn't trust herself to glance at him and hoped he saw her small gesture.

"In part we were right. They've focused their attention on the big guns – the rare artefacts and special exhibitions. The patrols have also been given explicit instructions to focus their time walking those areas and monitoring them. The bad news is they're still doing a quick pass through the corridors and section we need to infiltrate and they've doubled the rotations. Instead of having one pair of guards walk the halls every half hour, now there's the three pairs of guards doing the rounds every quarter hour."

"Surely spreading themselves that thin would mean they'd hurry through the dead zones – the sections we've mapped for – and be more alert in the so-called higher risk areas?" David suggested.

Kent made a 'so-so' face.

"We can't rely on that," he insisted. "Luke and I watched four rotations before coming here. It did appear they hurried through our sections – it's a lot of ground to cover in only fifteen minutes. And the guards are talking amongst themselves, sharing stories and bragging about who was where when the attempt went down earlier today. So they're distracted as we'd hoped. But our window is small. Worryingly small."

"Actually it might work in our favour," Chelsea suggested. She leant forward onto the table, resting on her elbows so her words weren't loud enough to carry far. "We'd already decided Thaddeus would remain outside to use a frontal attack as distraction – I saw first-hand how impressive that was this morning. Then when Kent and Luke are inside and give the signal I can jam the security cameras, which will add another level of distraction and disorientation."

"If our window is about fifteen minutes," David picked up, seeming to understand where she wanted to head, "then we can meet in the middle, at the painting. That way we've both got back-up should we run into a patrol team—four against six is much more even odds. Better yet, we can split up to escape, which will heighten our odds of success."

Kent seemed to think about this for a moment.

"The plan was always for you two to remain out of sight, monitoring the cameras and security system. That really is a job in and of itself."

"That's busy work to keep us occupied," Chelsea pointed out. "And you know it. We need a man on the outside, particularly Thaddeus, since he can cover our escapes and draw attention from the fact that we're already inside and successfully taking what we want. His role is crucial."

"Having someone monitor the level of our penetration and success, making certain they're not aware we've been inside until we're long gone, is also crucial." Luke weighed into the discussion.

Chelsea looked at the man and nodded.

"I agree, but I can do that while David and I give support to you and Kent."

She reached her hand into her bag and withdrew a small, thin laptop. The width of the computer was only a little bigger than the span of her palm. She held it so they could all see the device.

"This isn't exactly a brick, you know. The current book I'm reading is bigger and nearly twice as heavy. Everything I need to jam the cameras, monitor the alarm systems and watch our arses is on here. I don't need to be stationary to do my job."

Kent seemed intrigued. He cast a look at Thaddeus and Luke, finally looking between her and David.

"Look, if you really don't trust us by now, what are we doing here?" Chelsea asked with exasperation.

This was a gamble, but her instinct told her it was the right time to play it. After all the tests, the subtle barbs and the time they'd spent getting this far she felt a spurt of impatience was long overdue.

"David and I can be helpful here, as decoys if nothing else. You'll still have the art folder and take the canvas itself. No one here is disputing that. But if we come across a glitch or a problem — and, despite all our plans, the probability of that is high — then being able to split the team up and force security to scramble after us is an edge we should use."

"Okay," Kent relented with a nod. He moved the paper with the outline of the Gallery into the middle of the table and indicated a spot with his index finger. "This is how it will be. Thad, you will be in the same position, shooting distance with a clear range of the front of house. They've set up barricades here, here and across here. The street will be down to a crawl, bottlenecked to make things manageable for the police and made worse by the rubber-necking. As long as you stay in contact with us and make a lot of noise the rest is up to you."

Thaddeus smiled, a scary look in his eyes. Chelsea felt the man was having far too much fun, and not in a pleasant way. She hoped no one would get killed when he was finally let loose.

"Chelsea and David will neutralise the alarms at this point," Kent continued as he pointed to another section of the diagram. "Luke and I will be over here, waiting for your signal that we're clear to go. Chelsea will kill the cameras, and only then switch off the alarm as the security patrols panic. With luck, the loss of the visual surveillance and the noise of Thad's attack out front will take a minute or two for them to realise the system is fully down and not merely under attack. The four of us enter, and make our way directly to the Cézanne. That reminds me."

Kent unzipped a small outer pocket on his back pack and removed five small buds. When he handed them to each of them in turn Chelsea saw it was a small earpiece.

"They're all linked and we're on channel nine, the usual wavelength. Put them in but don't turn them on until we split up outside. Any last questions?"

"Yeah," Thaddeus drawled. "When do I get my cut?"

"We're meeting the Boss down by the docks at three a.m.," Kent replied. "Chelsea and David want to offer him a proposition of setting up their own crew, to start working independently but in line with the rest of us. If you want to come along you can, otherwise I'll wire the funds tomorrow morning once the banks open. It's up to you."

"There's nothing new with the exchange." Thaddeus sniffed. "I'd rather bang my girl. I'll expect the money before lunchtime."

Kent nodded, seeming satisfied with the large man's bored response.

"Anything else?" He glanced at them all, then stood when no one said anything and collected the paper from the table, folding it and putting it in his pocket. "Then let's move."

Chelsea stood, David right beside her. Nerves and excitement vied for attention as adrenaline surged through her body. It was crunch time. They were committed and really about to break into the London Gallery, steal a Cézanne and with luck later this evening finally discover the remaining member of this group and close it all down.

"Here we go," David murmured so only she could hear. Chelsea glanced at him, her eyes dancing. She smiled, not willing to say anything just yet and possibly jinx the situation.

He appeared to understand, winking at her. Warmth flooded her chest and she looked away before the others could sense the new intimacy flowing between them. They left the pub and the cool air of the night slapped her in the face. Chelsea sucked in a hasty breath and blinked hard against the icy coldness. She focused on the task ahead of her, getting her head back into the game.

Much as she adored David, this was not the time to be distracted.

Chapter Six

"Are you ready yet?" Kent's voice grumbled in her ear. Chelsea sighed silently, struggling to keep the annoyance out of her tone.

"As you pointed out when you hired me, this is a complex system. I'm nearly there, just give me a minute."

"The guards at the barricades are bored," Thaddeus added. "More than half of them are having a smoke, three have recently been delivered coffee — or someone ducked out and got them some. Looks like most of them are doing this for the overtime, not because they love the work."

"Means it's likely they'll scatter and desert the moment the noise begins," David suggested.

"You let Thad worry about that," Kent snapped, clearly cranky.

"Okay, I'm ready to disable the cameras," Chelsea interjected before Kent could lose his temper further. "Are we confirmed?"

"Do it."

Chelsea typed in the final commands and the internal video surveillance cameras she'd hacked into scrambled and went offline—now showing nothing but snow. Quickly she opened up the feed she'd linked into the alarm systems.

"Cameras are down. Thaddeus, you're cleared to start the distraction whenever you're—" Her words were cut off by an enormous boom of a heavy sounding explosion finishing the sentence for her.

"I'm in the alarm system," she continued, not wanting Kent's twitchiness and volatile temper to lead to paranoia. "Sections three and five are down...and seven... Okay, we're good to go. We need to remain clear of the main gallery, the large viewing room and the rotunda. Otherwise the place is ours."

"Entering now," Kent snapped.

Chelsea kept her laptop in hand, knowing she'd need to frequently check to make certain that the alarms remained off and that the cameras didn't get back online. David was already working on unlocking the side entrance. She remained silent, letting him work in peace. A moment later the lock clicked and he opened the door for her.

"Thanks," she said, entering first and glancing up and down the hallway. It was deserted.

"You should get your weapon," David commented. Chelsea wrinkled her nose, but obeyed. She unzipped a compartment in her bag and drew out her gun, checking it before they continued.

"I don't like having my hands full," she complained. With her gun in one hand and the laptop in the other she felt more vulnerable than if she hadn't got the gun.

"If we run into trouble I'd rather you had something for protection," David insisted. She nodded, knowing what he meant, but since she had no intention of killing anyone tonight it still rankled that her hands were full right then.

Not wanting to argue she remained silent and followed as David led them along the route they'd planned. All along they'd hoped to come along this far, not wanting to be left behind. They walked quickly, the corridors and labyrinth of passages long ago memorised.

Chelsea froze at the echo of gunfire through her earpiece.

"What's happening?" she asked, glancing down to her laptop screen. The cameras were still down, the alarms off.

"Nothing," Luke answered. "We just ran into a pair of security. Surprised them — they were on their way back to base, as we'd hoped."

Chelsea winced, hoping the men hadn't been killed but knowing she couldn't ask.

When she exchanged a speaking look with David, he recognised her concern, reached out a hand and tenderly touched her cheek. "It'll be okay," he mouthed.

She nodded, straightened her spine and jerked her chin ahead, indicating that they needed to keep moving.

Rushing now, she had to jog to keep up with him. They'd both known all along it was quite likely that people would die, but hearing that gunfire and the continual attack Thaddeus was waging outside made it all too real.

Steeling herself, Chelsea hurried, knowing the sooner they left the building the safer everyone else would be.

Only a few minutes later she and David stood at the doorway of the room where the Cézanne was kept. A large banner that read 'Where did they start?' hung across the doorway. The room inside was empty.

"Kent, we're here, where are you?"

"Just a minute." Another few shots rang out, both in her earpiece and from just down the corridor they'd come from. Chelsea turned in the direction of the sound, but already Luke had rounded the corner and was running towards them, his gun aimed in their direction.

David moved directly between Luke and Chelsea. She lifted her hand and placed it on David's shoulder. Part of her wanted to move him aside, protect him even as he covered her. She was caught somewhere between a girlish fluttering that he'd use his body as a shield and exasperation that he'd so willingly risk his life — which was so important to her — with such casual ease.

The point was moot. As Luke came closer to them he lowered his gun, not even breathing hard. He glanced up and down the hallway, checking for more guards. Kent strolled around the corridor as if he was on an innocent walk through the park.

"Good to see you didn't start without us," Kent said.

"The plan's for you and Luke to leave with the painting," Chelsea replied in what she hoped sounded like a bored tone. "We're sticking to the plan, right?"

"Of course," Kent replied mildly. Chelsea knew deep in her gut that she could trust this man almost as far as she could throw him — maybe not even that much.

Kent strode into the room, Luke covering his back and directly behind him. Chelsea glanced at David and raised her eyebrows.

"Obviously this is his moment," David commented wryly and in a low tone. Chelsea nodded. David waved an arm, indicating that she should enter before him. Knowing he'd argue the point should she explain she wanted to protect him as much as he her, she understood that protest would be useless and would merely waste time.

She entered the room, David protectively close.

Kent held a large artist's folder, one of those canvas, zip-up portfolios with cardboard sides that art students use to carry around their works in progress. Standing in front of the painting, Kent admired it, clearly enthralled. Luke stood beside him, back to the masterpiece, gazing around as if he expected armed mercenaries to come from the ceilings or through the windows at any moment. He held his arm high, the gun perfectly steady. Chelsea found it intriguing that the man didn't even glance at the artwork around him.

Situated in the middle of the wall, at perfect viewing level, and lit by a number of discreetly placed spotlights embedded into the plaster, the picture was darkly sensual. Bold greens and browns showed a park or country woodland style setting, with a few couples scattered a distance away picnicking and enjoying each other's company.

The main characters in the picture were front and centre, drawn in intricate detail. A blonde Caucasian woman was clasped in the embrace of an olive-skinned, dark-haired man. They were both utterly naked.

At first glance Chelsea thought the painting was strangely romantic, the evident passion in the embrace and the undressed state of the couple hinting at an underlying sexuality. Upon closer inspection Chelsea realised that the woman leant back, her upflung arms not necessarily the posture of a woman giving herself over to sensuality, but perhaps actually struggling with an attacker.

Divided, in the minute or so she had to assess the tableau before her, she truly couldn't decide whether it was a sensual, darkly erotic scene or one with more sinister, rape-like undertones. Clearly it would be a matter of personal interpretation, and in that moment she could instantly understand how one could look for hours upon the scene and debate what it truly depicted.

She began to understand why someone might want to possess such a rich, complicated piece of art.

A small ping came from her laptop.

Chelsea thrust her gun into the compartment of her bag. She lifted her computer and typed a few quick keystrokes. She groaned.

"What is it?" Kent snapped. Already he had moved directly in front of the painting and was preparing to lift it down from the wall.

"I don't understand," she murmured, typing as quickly as possible with one hand. "Section three is up and running again. Someone must be in the system, here on site."

"Get it down again," Kent insisted.

Ignoring him and his surly attitude she tried to corrupt the security system permanently. Balancing the success of the mission with causing the least damage, she'd originally been reluctant to truly have the Gallery offline and in need of major repair. If someone with better skills than she was there and threatening the mission, however, she'd do whatever was necessary.

As she delved deeper into the code, she noticed time stamps on some of the systems and folders she scrolled past.

"Damn, someone is here, upgrading the system," she explained as the situation became clear. "Hurry up, Philippe, our small window just closed. I'm good, but I'm a grafter, an inside person. Hacking is just an interesting hobby. If this guy is a professional I can only delay him, not stop him."

"Do it," Kent grunted as he lifted the painting down from the wall. Chelsea didn't know if he meant shut the upgrade guy down, or corrupt the system, or something else, and in part she didn't care. Clearly his attention remained predominantly on the artwork.

Dividing her attention between holding off the man trying to get the alarms and cameras back up and running, and Kent, she winced as he destroyed the gorgeous antique frame surrounding the painting. Wood splintered with a crack that sounded eerily similar to breaking bone.

With a care she hadn't seen him use with anything else, he removed the canvas from the frame and transferred it into his folder. Chelsea tried to shut down the surveillance as soon as the sections were up and running, but she knew it was a losing battle.

"He's reached our section," she warned. "If we're unlucky they can see us now."

"Then it's time to go," Kent said, his tone far friendlier now he had what he wanted. "We'll go back through the amateurs and section two—is that still down?"

"For now," she nodded, understanding what the bastard was doing. "But section five is up and that's the only other—"

"You said the reason you wanted to come along was distraction, so go be one," Kent said.

Chelsea sighed as Kent and Luke hurried out of the room. Snapping her laptop shut, she then shoved it into her bag, pulled out her gun and spare ammo and zipped her pack tightly shut. Grateful for the pockets in her jeans, she crammed spare clips front and back, checked her gun and looked at her lover with a wry grin.

"This is fun, right?" she asked dryly. "Shooting our way out of the National Gallery, hoping to not kill innocent people who have every intention of killing us while that backstabbing arsehole takes the coward's way out?"

David chuckled, seeming cool and not fazed in the least.

"You wanted excitement, darling," he pointed out. She threw her head back and laughed, chambering a round in her gun. She felt better with a hand free, the balance of her small pack an easy, almost comforting weight.

"Come on, let's go kick some butt and finish this," she said. "I'll take point, you watch our arse, and no heroics this time. We're going to have a long discussion about you putting yourself between a cocked gun and me."

"Instinct," David replied blithely as they left the room and turned in the direction opposite to that from which they'd come earlier. "My mother bred a gentleman, don't you know."

"You're a chivalrous man to your fingertips," she agreed as they ran hard. "But I'm not some quivering, virginal innocent untrained in the fighting arts. Besides, I want to protect you with an equal intensity."

The sound of gunfire came from a neighbouring corridor, distracting her. Chelsea dropped the discussion and swore.

"This way." David took her free hand and tugged her down a different hallway. For a second she baulked.

"That leads to the main gallery — "

"I think the quickest route will be best just now," David insisted. "Chances are our friends have all the internal systems back up and running. Faster is better right now."

Realising he was right, she let him tug her forward and together they sprinted. They ran past sculptures and priceless works of art, glass cabinets showcasing rare pieces of ancient jewellery and weapons of war. She ignored them all, focused purely on their escape.

"Halt!" a deep voice boomed from in front of them. Chelsea sighed, knowing it would have been too much to hope that they wouldn't be confronted. David stood beside her, his gun raised. Their shoulders pressed together as they faced off against the four men.

"Lower your weapons," the guard insisted.

"We can't do that, mate," David replied coolly.

Chelsea remained silent, assessing the four security men. Two appeared hardened, determined. She was shocked that they had guns. Part of her mind decided they must be some of the newer recruits after the false alarm this morning. Mercenaries, perhaps. Their postures and shooting stance indicated they'd been in the military.

They'd be problematic.

The other two were younger, clearly new to the job, and possibly in their first confrontation. Neither held weapons, only batons. Unless directly confronted in close quarters Chelsea didn't see either man being a problem.

It rubbed her the wrong way to kill or seriously injure such men. They were all merely doing their job, responding to a breech in security. She and David were doing their jobs, trying to fight the good fight, but she couldn't find it in her to kill these men.

"Lower your weapons or you'll force our hands," one of the military men snapped out insistently.

"Older guy's thighs," Chelsea whispered to David. There was a pause of about a second while he seemed to think about her request. Then with a single nod of his head they both fired.

Chelsea started with one of the more seasoned men. She shot once, catching her target in the upper thigh on her second round. It was undoubtedly painful, but in the fleshy part of his leg. While the wound bled, it didn't gush and she breathed a sigh of relief.

He went down with a grunt, hit, but nothing vital or not easily repaired. David had only needed the one shot. Both the military men were on the floor, effectively disarmed. Both the younger guards had instantly raised their hands in the global gesture of surrender the moment they'd fired.

David waved his gun, indicating for the men to step aside, which they did with haste.

"Throw your communications into the corner over here," David shouted harshly. "Walkie-talkies, earpieces, the lot. Now, or the next lot won't be in your thighs."

There was a pregnant pause. David and Chelsea simultaneously cocked their weapons, the sound echoing clearly across the room. The other men obeyed, the equipment hitting the parquet floor with a clank.

David and Chelsea edged around the chamber, placing as much distance as possible between themselves and the guards. David dropped and picked up some of the units in a quick motion. Just as they reached the doorway another shot rang out. Chelsea's heart leapt to her throat, fear pounding in her veins.

One of the ex-military men had lifted himself onto his shoulder, his face twisted in pain and his black pants soaked with wetness. His gun was lifted and directed at David. Her shoulder was grabbed, David held her tightly. He growled in her ear.

"Run, now!"

Chelsea reached out her free hand and gripped David's shirt, refusing to let him go.

"How bad are you?" she snapped out, fear causing adrenaline to surge and her tone to sound far harsher than she intended. They both ran full tilt for the front entrance and escape.

"What?" David said, his attention clearly diverted. "Just hold on, we're almost there."

Everything became confusing. Chelsea felt that she was missing something. David's words didn't make sense to her. Was he delirious?

Puffing now, she was surprised how draining she found their run, coupled with the fear and heart-pounding surge of adrenaline.

The columns of the Gallery's outer entrance loomed ahead of her as they crossed the enormous front foyer. It seemed strange, almost unbelievable that only twelve or so hours ago she'd been walking inside across this very floor when a rocket launcher had decimated the outside.

She giggled, and wondered if hormones and her body's reaction to the stress were making her hysterical.

"Just a little longer," David said. "You can make it, love."

"Of course I can," she insisted, not understanding what he was talking about. Only a dozen paces from the front doors she saw numerous men racing backwards and forwards in a dizzying manner.

"Well, we did want distractions." She chuckled, not quite certain why she found it so funny to watch. There was an enormous fire out on the street. It took a moment for her to realise one of the security jeeps was burning.

"Those will be Thad's missiles," she said.

David grabbed her arm, halting her before they could push through the doors. Without a word he took the earpiece out of her ear and replaced it with one of the ones he'd taken from the guards they'd shot.

"Clip this to your belt," he said, handing her a walkie-talkie as he removed their crew's earpiece and replaced it with a stolen one. "Now, act hurt. Turn your shoulder so everyone can see the blood."

"Sure. I'm...hey, what?"

Chelsea looked down to her arm, shocked to see a dark, wet stain covering most of the slender limb. Pain rolled over her, like being hit in the face with a bat.

"Holy fuck, that arsehole shot me."

David opened the door and turned when she didn't immediately follow him. He reached out and tenderly took the hand of her unhurt arm. As he tugged her, she noticed the worry and fear etched onto his face. She felt sick to her stomach, certain for one horrifying moment that she was going to throw up everywhere in an ignoble fashion and ruin her reputation.

Her mouth opened, but no words came to her lips. Shock — cold and heavy — blanketed her body, the pain of her shoulder beating at her.

"Darling," David crooned to her, urgency underlying his gentle tone. "I know what to do, please trust me, but we have to move. Now. Please, love."

Chelsea breathed deeply, surprised at how the simple act made her shudder. She let him lead her, willing her feet to move. It took an immense amount of mental power to force her body to react. She'd often heard how fear could freeze a soldier, that terror killing almost as many warriors as any other weapon.

Until this moment she'd pooh-poohed the idea, not understanding how shock could literally take over your will and body with such force.

"That's it," David urged her warmly. "Let's go. I'll get you patched up. You're fine."

The tone of his voice more than the actual words gave her strength. David kept his face on her, his gaze steady, giving her the stimulation she needed to gain momentum once again. She pushed the pain from her mind, compartmentalising it. She'd scream bloody murder later, she promised herself. Right now they had to live, to escape and finish the mission. As they moved, walking a slow trek down the flight of stairs and past the crumbled pillars, heading towards the burning car, her energy gradually returned.

"I'm okay," she insisted, though her tone was thready and faint.

"Of course you are," David replied, clearly not believing a word. A shout rose up as they were noticed. Chelsea trembled in fear, certain they were about to be shot — or, worse, arrested. She did not want to explain their last-minute fuck-up to McIlroy or the London branch of the Agency.

"I've got you," David said in a low tone, just to her. He then turned his head to the group of guards heading their way and shouted in a commanding tone.

"We're on Murphy's team. We were just ambushed in the Eastern corridor in section five, two hostiles. Murphy and the others are down but alive but I need a medic here — my partner's been shot."

David pulled the walkie-talkie from his belt and lifted it at the men, his head turned so they could see the earpiece they'd all been issued. Relaxing, half the men turned around and returned to their post. Two came closer.

"We heard about that, but then we lost contact. What the fuck is going on in there?"

"I have no idea," David insisted, still steadily leading Chelsea towards the barriers and their freedom. "We were attacked, exchanged fire. They're on the run, though. The two we saw weren't carrying anything. I think we got to them before they achieved their goal. My partner needs attention, though. Where are the medics?"

The guards waved over to the far side of the street. Chelsea could see the flashing lights of an ambulance.

"Thanks," she said faintly, pain clear in her tone. The guards nodded and let them pass without further comment.

David and Chelsea made a beeline for the ambulance, leaving the hectic insanity of the Gallery behind. The guards all but ignored them now, focused on what was occurring inside, talking on their radios and trying to make contact. Once they'd passed the barriers and roadblocks David cast a brief glance behind them.

"Okay, we need to jog—not run, but move fast. Will you be all right?"

"I'm fine," Chelsea insisted. In truth she felt shaky, but damned if she'd let David carry her out on his back—which she knew he would, should it come to that. Her legs wobbled dangerously at the thought of running, but she forced her self-doubt down. She could do this.

"You lead, I'll follow," she promised him.

He cast her a worried look, but didn't comment further. David took her hand, holding her in a firm but steady grip. "This way," he said, and they set off.

The street around them blurred. All Chelsea could focus upon was remaining upright and placing one foot in front of the other as quickly as possible. David led them both between cars parked at all kinds of angles—diagonally across the street and some even half up on the footpath. She found the pain in her arm was moving down the side of her torso, sending shots of agony burning along her body and into her stomach. Chelsea pressed her lips tightly together, refusing to make a sound that would distract David.

Breathing heavily through her nose, she found by focusing on David she gave herself something to think of beside the pain and her wobbly legs. David swivelled his head like a damn motion detector. Left to right, right to left, left to right, back and forth. It took her an astonishing amount of time to understand that he was surveying around them, making certain they didn't draw unwanted attention.

Guilt beat at her for a moment. She was dragging him down, a liability. She was putting his life and safety at risk.

"David," she panted, shocked at how wheezy and thin her voice was. She gasped for air, wanting to tell him he needed to run and get away, finish this and put Thaddeus, Luke, Kent and whoever the main Boss they answered to was away in jail for life. She could just sit quietly in some nice dark corner and happily pass out.

David's gaze rested momentarily on her, but then he continued to jog outside the perimeter that had been set up around the Gallery.

"We're close," he promised. "Do you need me to carry you?"

"No!" she protested as strongly as possible. "You should go, hurry. The docks."

Further speech was beyond her, the pain intensifying.

"You better hope that's the shock talking there," David said grimly. "If I was the one shot and you leading us to safety, would you ditch me?"

Chelsea sighed, too exhausted to admit he was right. Pain beat at her, but if she were honest she'd carry David to hell and back out again if necessary. She narrowed her mental focus to the running, too winded to speak more. On some subconscious level it depressed her that she was too exhausted and drained to even argue. That alone told her how low she'd been brought.

Her injured arm had gone numb, thankfully. A part of her mind knew that wasn't a good thing, but the temporary relief overshadowed any worry she could muster.

It could have been minutes or half an hour later when David led her into a small alley. Chelsea had lost track not only of where they were, but also of the time. Heaving to catch her breath, she leaned against the brick wall while David upturned an old crate.

"Sit down," he said gently and helped her to sit. "I need to call the others, make sure they're safe and the exchange is still happening on the docks at two."

"What's the time?" she panted. It cost her to focus, was unbelievably difficult, but she forced herself.

"We've got time. It's only half past midnight."

Chelsea leaned her head back against the bricks, her eyes fluttering shut. Pain washed over her and she let it beat against her senses, hoping that she could let the worst of it pass before they needed to move again. She heard the sound of a zipper, then the faint *click, click* as David typed in a number on his phone.

"Phillipe? Yeah, it's Greer here. Chelsea and I are out. You both got away with the package?"

There was a pause. Chelsea was too tired to try to eavesdrop further. That would have required moving, and energy — things she wasn't keen on just then.

"Chelsea's been hit. It's not serious, but I want it taken care of before the exchange. Are the details the same?"

There was another short pause before David wrapped it up. "Okay, we'll see you then."

"If he can stab us in the back, he will," she murmured. David pressed a palm to her forehead, his touch beyond tender.

"He's already effectively proven so," David replied, "when he made us take the harder route out. He's a coward, exactly as you warned. Don't worry, I won't be trusting him — you have my word."

"How far are we from the car?"

"Only a few streets over. I have anti-inflammatories and some hard-core painkillers at my place. I'm worried about your fever, though. Do you have medical contacts here? This would be an awful time to ask favours from the London office, but I'd deal with Lucifer himself if I had to."

Chelsea frowned. She had a fever? Lifting her head, she waited a moment, then sat forward on the crate, only to feel her top sticking to her back where sweat had dampened the material.

"Is there an exit wound?" she asked, concerned for the first time.

The light in the alley was atrocious, and when David bent her a few degrees more forward pain shot like fire across her back. She cut her cry off almost the second it had escaped her mouth, but she'd rarely seen such concern in David's dark eyes.

"The bullet is still in you somewhere. Thank fuck that arsehole aimed high. Your wound is right up the top of your chest, just below your collarbone. Small calibre, the blood has already clotted and stopped itself. I'm sure you'll have a glorious scar, but it can't have hit anything important. But the shock, your sweating and general disorientation have me terrified you'll run the risk of infection. We might need to call in a favour."

Chelsea shook her head.

"We don't have time to mess around with codes and making calls. Do you have tools at your place?" David was silent. Chelsea groaned impatiently. "David, I trust you. I'd far rather have you digging around in my body extracting a bullet than some random bloody stranger who might call other agents to isolate and contain us rather than take our word."

"I've got the tools," he said with evident reluctance. Chelsea sagged back, wrung dry.

"Then lead the way."

Chapter Seven

David had never felt anything remotely to what he'd experienced in the last fifteen minutes. Chelsea had fluttered in and out of consciousness on the drive back to his rented flat. While part of him had craved running every red light and speeding like a demon, logic had dictated that with the police on alert and the Gallery partially in flames and ruins, now would not be an ideal time to be caught breaking such a mundane law. Particularly not when his travelling companion was a black-clad, beautiful woman with a bullet lodged in her shoulder.

Some things were difficult to explain.

He'd ended up carrying her into the flat, wild with worry. Her porcelain skin was flushed and damp from sweat. Her top was swimming in her blood. Should she need a transfusion he'd break down and call the Agency—rules and the final link be damned. Chelsea's life came before the mission. She'd chew him out for it later, but he'd bear that if it meant she'd be here to do so.

After laying her down on his bed, he'd first given her an injection of morphine. The sting of the needle had roused her, though she was still groggy.

"Forgive me, darling," he'd pleaded and urged her to bite down on his belt. Her gorgeous eyes had widened, understanding what she'd woken up for, putting a look of fear in her he sincerely hoped to never see again.

Digging the bullet out of her shoulder had been the hardest task he'd ever had to do. The morphine had taken the edge off, but he knew he'd hurt her. Near the end she'd passed out, and he felt grateful for that.

Now, after wetting a washcloth from a basin of warm water, he cleaned her wound. Already a giant, ugly bruise marred her delicate skin.

"I'm going to stitch this for you in a minute," he spoke to her. Even though she wasn't conscious he hoped that the sound of his voice would calm her, be with her wherever her mind currently dwelt. "If you hadn't shown such compassion, chances are good I'd have killed both those dangerous men and this wouldn't have happened. Proof for you, darling, that no good deed goes unpunished. I'll just be one second."

Laying the basin and bloodstained cloth on his bedside table, David went back into the bathroom. His emergency medical kit was open, paraphernalia spread out everywhere. Neatness had not been his concern earlier, nor was he fussed now. He broke the wrapping on a sterilised needle and bit open a packet of surgeon's thread.

The bullet wound was nasty, but not huge. With luck he could close it with three, maybe four stitches. It had been a long time since he'd had to do this himself, but it was not a skill one forgot easily.

When he returned to the bedroom Chelsea was murmuring, though still clearly unconscious. Making the mental note that next time he'd make certain he carried some liquid antibiotics he could inject when necessary, he was careful not to rouse her. Chelsea was one of the strongest women he'd ever encountered, but watching someone stitch up your torn flesh was not a particularly pleasant memory. He'd rather shield her from it if he could.

He laboriously, carefully closed the wound with precise, careful moves. Finished, he heaved a sigh of relief. Lastly, he returned to the bathroom, picked up a glass of water, some antibiotic pills and antiseptic gel. When he dabbed the gel onto the raw skin with a wadded tissue, the sting from the iodine roused her again.

At first she looked at him with confusion, but memory returned swiftly. Chelsea glanced at his face, then around the practically barren room.

"I hope your home has a bit more décor than this," she murmured. Her humour had returned. David felt something that had been tightly knotted within him ease.

"My home is a sensual, lush paradise you will crave to never leave," he joked. As hoped, she chuckled.

When she moved her shoulder carefully, she winced at the motion. "I can't explain it, but it feels better even though it's more painful."

"The body senses when it has a foreign object in it," he said seriously. "You've heard of the healthy pain of a cleanly broken bone, rather than a messy shattering or being stabbed? This is similar. Here, take these."

He held the glass of water and pills out to her. She took them without hesitation, sipped the water and swallowed the tablets.

"Antibiotics," he said, even though she didn't ask. Her faith and trust warmed him anew.

"How much longer do we have?" she asked.

David glanced at her. He'd cut her shirt off with scissors, not willing to hurt her further or spare the time to remove her top any other way. Blood still stained much of her skin—though her wound now was perfectly clean. She no longer sweated from the physical taxation of running or being on her feet.

Summed up, Chelsea appeared drawn, tired and shaky, but fine.

Part of him wanted her to remain there, safe and preferably asleep so she could heal. He doubted she'd do either of those without an almost fight—one that would further drain her reserves. In particular, he knew her well enough to understand that if she could feel the strength of her second wind coming to her, she'd understandably want to see this to the end.

"We have a short while before I have to leave," he said. Chelsea winced as she sat up. David instinctively reached behind her and lifted the pillows to support her back, knowing this would not be pretty.

"Are we going to have our first serious argument?" he asked, ruthlessly using his lilting accent in the hopes of staving off or distracting this stubborn woman beside him.

"Of course not," she replied. He wasn't taken in by the innocent look she gave him, obviously no more than she was distracted by his accent.

"We're partners, aren't we? Equals?" she said.

David hesitated before responding, feeling the trap close around him but at a loss on how to stop it before he was stuck. "Yeeeees," he drew the word out, searching mentally for a way out.

"And we've always been side by side on this journey. It's our mission. Not mine. Not yours. That's how we started and have progressed for over eighteen months now. Together."

"You've been shot, sickened by blood loss and—"

"I'm a big girl," Chelsea insisted. "This'll be a few hours, maximum. We go to the docks, we meet with Kent and Luke and this final figure, and hand over the painting. We have some bullshit discussion to argue our right to start a new crew. We get photos, a voice recording, and then we're out. McIlroy can organise for some other poor bastards to shadow the three guys. Maybe we help later for them to run down Thaddeus, though I'm sure McIlroy is already well on top of that. Then we're done. We take a well-earned vacation alone together—I'm partial to warmer climates and the beach, just so you know—and screw each other in every conceivable position on the sandy beach. Am I missing something?"

David sighed. He sat on the corner of the bed and took her hand in his. He caught her gaze and held it for a long moment.

"And what if something goes wrong?" he asked in a soft tone. "What if this boss of Phillipe's thinks we're moles, or that it's the trap it actually is? What if he has back-up, people willing to shoot at us? You're not at your best, darling. It'd be a risk even if you were a hundred per cent healthy. A cornered animal is always the more vicious one. You know this."

"And knowing that," she continued, "do you really think I'd let you face the three of them alone? Phillip has already let us fend for ourselves twice in less than twenty-four hours. Do you honestly expect me to lie here and be sick, or to rest while you go out there and face them alone? Either your brains are addled with sleep deprivation and worry, or you don't begin to comprehend the depths to which I love you. You're not the only person here who treasures their partner. I'm not immune to that tone in your voice, the accent you're stressing right now, or the heat of your eyes, the worry and love I can see in your every movement. I feel all that back at you and more."

David couldn't begin to reply to that. What could he say? She watched him, her heart and soul bared in her eyes and offered practically to him on a plate and waved under his nose. How could he possibly knock it back?

"I could tie you to the bed." He grinned, tempted but mostly teasing. Sort of. She chuckled, tugged his hand to bring him closer. She tilted her head, her lips just inches from his.

"If you tie me to this bed," she purred, throwing his words back at him, "then you bloody well better be sticking around to use it to good purpose. I'm not some delicate, fainting virginal miss. If you bring out those guns, Mister, you better follow it up with hard, exotic actions."

"You'd give me that much control?" he asked, surprised. Chelsea was a wanton, wickedly delightful woman. But he'd not have guessed for her to be up for those sorts of games. She grinned, a tiny dimple flashing at the corner of her mouth.

"Within limits I'd do anything for you," she agreed. "If you wanted to test those waters I'd be more than willing. Using such methods to keep me here while you faced danger alone and undefended, with no real back-up — now that's a different breed of beast and I'd make sure you lived to regret it."

Knowing defeat when he faced it, David nodded. In this situation he figured it would be better to accept with grace than be hog-tied on the floor still kicking and screaming.

"Let's make certain you're up for it then," he conceded. He tilted her chin, lowered his head and kissed her tenderly. He moved his hands lower, stroking over her bloodstained skin, taking great care to give a wide berth to her wound and the nasty bruise the force of the bullet lodging in her had left.

As he stroked his fingers over her bra-covered nipples, he loved the moan she gave. A small tremor shook her body and David quickly removed his hands, then sat on them. He slowly pulled his lips away from hers, hating the loss of warmth and contact.

"I don't want you to stop," she complained. He pressed a kiss to the tip of her nose and moved back on the mattress.

"You need me to stop," he countered. "Your body has been taxed enough. You might not feel it yet, but I bet you're a lot more exhausted than you realise. Come on, stand up and let's go to the bathroom. While you wash up in the basin I'll find another shirt for you to wear. It will have to be one of mine, I'm afraid."

He assisted her in getting up from the bed. David could see it bothered her in the annoyed set to her mouth. Being so weak and reliant rubbed her the wrong way, but at first her moves were stiff. Chelsea flexed her legs, stretched her muscles and warmed up a bit, her innate grace returning. Her upper body remained rigid, the pain evident, but apparently manageable.

When Chelsea made her way to the bathroom he grabbed two shirts that were slightly smaller than the others and followed her, hooking them over the doorknob.

"Took a bit of a beating," Chelsea commented. David watched her. She appeared calm, but he could see deeper. He thought this might be the first time she truly understood just how much damage she'd taken and how lucky she'd been. A few inches lower and things could have been very different.

"You can change your mind at any time," he offered her. She cast him an angry glance that seared him.

"Let's not go over that again," she warned. She picked up one of his hair elastics and handed it to him. When he worked he often pulled his hair back into a short ponytail. Lately, though, he'd become used to wearing it down since that's how Chelsea seemed to enjoy it. He took the elastic and raised an eyebrow at her.

"I love your hair," she commented. "But it's distracting. You usually tie it up when we're not relaxing, and I think of it as your focused persona. I'd rather keel over than admit to the pain I'm feeling right now. My pride can't take another blow. But I will acknowledge that I'm not at my best at this moment. I don't want to be fantasising about your hair caressing my naked skin while I need my energy focused on the mission. I can't afford to be visualising how it felt when you were thrusting inside me, and those soft tendrils moved softly over my face. So, the hair tie."

A darkly sensual, very masculine part to him rose and roared its approval, pleased by the admission. He would have loved nothing better than to spread her wide on the bed, strip her naked and make long, slow, languid love to her. He'd brush his hair over every inch of her skin just as she wanted, then lick and kiss it again and again.

Sadly, that would have to wait.

He pulled his hair into a ponytail and tied it back.

Chelsea sighed, seeming torn between being pleased and sad, and returned to cleaning up.

"I'll get my phone. We need to give McIlroy the details and a heads-up," he said. She nodded and he left the room to go get his phone. Pulling it out of his small kit, he then turned the phone on, and dialled their boss's number. While the phone rang he walked back to the bathroom.

"Yeah?" McIlroy answered.

"It's Greer. Is this secure?"

"Yeah. What have you got? I've been on tenterhooks since we got your beep."

Chelsea turned to watch him as he entered the bathroom. He stood beside her, tilting the phone so she could hear everything.

"It's one of Cézanne's earlier works. A forest or garden scene with a white woman and an olive-skinned man embracing or fighting on a path. Subjective, but beautiful and brilliantly executed. We're meeting the Boss on the docks, down near the seedier side of Canary Wharf at three. There was a snag, though."

"Give me a moment," McIlroy said. David heard him dial a number on a different phone—McIlroy, he knew, often had three or even four at any given time for different high-priority missions. "Canary Wharf at three. We'll want a sharp shooter and a minimum of three teams circling to pick up the bogeys... Just get there, I'll call back with more details in a minute. You already have pictures of two of the targets, so it shouldn't be that hard."

"Right. Greer. I've already heard about the second attack on the Gallery. Do you realise the shit I'm going to be in tomorrow morning with London over all this?"

"You live for the politics and wrangling," David replied calmly. "As I was saying, we have a problem. Chelsea was shot."

"What?" McIlroy shouted. "You need to make this meeting. Almost two years will be down the drain if you can't identify this bloody Boss. We didn't even know he existed until the two of you went undercover. He's the reason I've accepted the length and cost of this whole mission. There's no sense cutting an arm off this group – we need to round them all up in one hit and this is the last link we need."

"I'm well aware of that," David replied frostily. "And if it were up to me I'd be going in alone. Chelsea, however, has other ideas. She's weak, but will be okay. We'll need that back-up, though, presumably the groups you just sent now. I need confirmation you can take it from the exchange onwards. We'll get your photos and voice print, and extract ourselves with our covers intact in case we need to reopen the investigation at a later date. But I'm telling you, McIlroy, you better have this sewn up tight, because once we egress the docks we're out on leave. For the full two weeks you owe us."

"Greer, you sew up this ring and you and Atchison can take three weeks off with my blessing."

"So you just need our call?" David checked.

"I've had teams on standby for the last few days, on amber light preparedness since you sent the beacon earlier today. All the Dublin and Cardiff rings are surrounded and being monitored, and the crew who will pick up Thaddeus, Luke and Kent are moving into position as we speak. Once we get a bead on this Boss, the central leader of all the smaller rings, then we'll be good to go."

"Great," David replied, pleased it was finally coming to a head. He cast a look at Chelsea, who nodded. She reached behind him and took the shirt he'd left on the doorknob and carefully began to push her arms into the sleeves, then slowly pulled it up over her head.

"Well then, I guess this is it. Make sure your team knows we can't be contacted until after we leave. Have they got eyes and ears?"

"They'll be able to listen to what you say, but not get a message to you. But they will be able to hear, so be as descriptive as you can without giving yourselves away."

"Will do. See you on the other side, McIlroy."

"Be safe."

David hung up the phone and switched it off. He turned to find Chelsea staring at him. He smiled at her.

"What?"

"Will they be able to see and hear us?" she asked him.

He nodded. "Yep, so if I figure as long as we're verbose but careful about it this should be fine. This is the last stage, darling. Then we get three weeks of that beach-side hot monkey sex you promised me."

She laughed, which was why he'd said it. Wrapping her in a warm hug, David held her close, loving the way she felt in his arms. He never wanted to let her go.

Sadly, reality and work called. Indulging for just a brief moment, he kissed her. His body heated, needing her with a growing intensity he hated to deny. When they were both breathless, he pulled back.

"Let's go," he said in a soft tone.

Chapter Eight

Chelsea pulled her jacket more tightly around her body, then winced as the action tugged painfully on her wound and stitches. She felt, rather than saw, David's gaze upon her.

"Bloody stitches," she complained.

Tiredness lapped at her. In truth, she was secretly grateful they wouldn't need to do any chasing or following tonight. Her energy reserves were depleted.

David closed his hand around hers, and for a wonderful moment she let herself draw strength from him. They walked down the Docklands, making their way to the meeting point. The night was bitterly cold, a breeze coming off the water and dropping the temperature another couple of degrees.

There'll be snow before too much longer, she figured.

"Should be just here, up ahead," David said. He squeezed her fingers one more time then let it go.

Chelsea glanced around, curious as to where the other agents might be. Out of sight, obviously, but they'd need to be near enough to follow at a moment's notice.

"Wonder what frequency they're on," she pondered idly. They rounded a corner and saw Luke and Kent. Not altering their pace, they made their way up to them. Phillipe still had the large artist's folder, presumably with the Cézanne inside it.

David made a minor show of checking his watch. They were almost exactly five minutes early.

"You guys been here long?" she asked.

Kent shook his head. "Couple of minutes. We wanted to check out the drop site."

Chelsea shrugged, a flicker crossing her face as even the movement of her good shoulder pulled slightly on her wound.

"How'd you both get out?"

"Wasn't hard," David said smoothly, sounding almost bored. "We walked out of the front door. Wish we'd been able to take photos. Was quite a scene Thaddeus left out there. Sections of the building crumbled, car on fire. Looked like his kind of party."

"He certainly appeared to have had fun," Kent agreed.

A silence descended between them. While not strained, it was not quite comfortable either. Chelsea had the impression that there were many things very consciously not being said—by all of them. Questions being restrained and accusations being kept in check.

After the first minute some of the tension seemed to ease.

"So you two want to take a crack on your own?" Luke asked. Chelsea nodded, remaining silent. David spoke up. They'd agreed she'd step in if things got too awkward, but for tonight he'd take the lead for the most part. Still pretty doped up on painkillers she wasn't at her intellectual best.

"We might fall flat on our face and come crawling back for work," he said. "But we're an...independent partnership. And we think we have plenty to offer. We'd like to at least make our case to the Boss, see what he has to say about it."

"So make your case," Luke replied.

Chelsea frowned, not understanding. She exchanged a look with David, who seemed equally puzzled.

"We don't need to justify ourselves to you, nor highlight our finer points," she said carefully.

Her instincts screamed caution to her. In no way did she want to pander to this man, but neither did she want to appear disrespectful. Something warned her there were currents of change around them, and until she had a complete handle on the situation she didn't want to burn any bridges. Besides, if possible they wanted to leave here with all their reputations intact, in case they needed these contacts at a later date.

"You've seen our work, seen what we're capable of and know our work ethic. We've been on the same crew for close to a year now. Anyway, it's not you we need to explain this to, it's Phillipe's Boss. If we needed to get your approval to strike out on our own we'd have done it weeks ago."

"I'm aware of that," Luke replied. "That's why I've been drawing this out. We needed your contacts and information inside the Gallery to make this heist. I couldn't risk you losing interest and carrying out something different. Added on to that, I just didn't trust either one of you. I'm still not a hundred per cent on board. Something about you both just sets my internal radar off."

Chelsea realised Luke was doing all the talking. Phillipe stood beside him, yes, and Phillipe carried the painting, but usually Luke was quiet if not silent.

Phillipe was the crew leader, Luke his friend and quasi-second in command.

She understood why the currents of power seemed different tonight. Phillipe was deferring to Luke, not the other way around. In a flash she put the pieces of the puzzle together, to create a startling larger picture.

"You're the Boss," David said, seeming to understand at the same time as her. "It's been you all along. Kent glances at you when delicate decisions are made. You use him as a mouthpiece."

"I don't use him," Luke demurred. "We simply let everyone see what they wish to. Kent is in truth the leader of his cell. He makes those calls. I just find it fun to keep my hand in the game on a more elemental level—I started out as a thief and find nothing gives me that same thrill and jolt of being somewhere I ought not. Situations like this, where I'm not completely on board with someone or a scenario, I find I can gather a lot more information being in the background, present but overlooked, rather than on display as 'the Boss'. It's a win-win situation really."

"Well then, you know us, obviously," Chelsea said. "What do you think?"

Chelsea tossed her hair back from her face, hoping that her sudden onset of nerves weren't betrayed by her tone or body language. She couldn't help but madly think back, wonder if there'd been even the slightest indication of something not being kosher. She didn't think she'd said or done anything embarrassing or wrong in Luke's presence, but so much of the time she'd overlooked him—focused on the larger picture—she couldn't be sure.

"I think...that I just can't trust you," Luke replied grimly as he pulled a large handgun from the small of his back.

Instantly, as it always did in the heat of battle, everything simultaneously sped up and slowed right down to a crawl.

They all pulled out guns, almost at identical times. Phillipe screamed out, "Thaddeus!" and Chelsea cringed.

The large blond man was fucking crazy. Knowing he was in the darkness somewhere, likely with half an arsenal and an eager grin on his face, she expected a flame-thrower to blast out any second now. She didn't let that stop her, however.

Focusing her sights on Phillipe, she thought of how casually he'd left her and David to fend for themselves in the Gallery, of how he'd blithely ordered Thad to attack the hell out of the place in broad daylight with hundreds of innocent tourists and schoolchildren scattered around.

Kent Phillipe was a bully and a coward. If she could only pull her trigger once, she wanted it to count. In the few seconds she had, she steadied her gaze, lined up her shot, and pulled the trigger. As she heard the explosion, saw the bullet hit its mark — his lower thigh, just above the kneecap — she watched him fall with no real sense of satisfaction. Indeed, she didn't feel much of anything except tiredness.

As if the world had come crashing back to her she heard bullets whizzing around her. David and Luke exchanged a volley of shots, Luke falling after a couple of seconds, clutching his chest. Before she could react or check if David was unharmed she heard the heavy sound of booted feet running towards them.

Whirling around, she then lifted her gun, fully expecting to see Thaddeus coming after them with some ungodly weapon drawn, about to fry them into ashes. Despite the fact that her heart thundered, and she genuinely thought she'd die in the next few seconds, she didn't have time to be afraid or regret how little time she'd been given to share with David.

A man whom she didn't recognise at all—not Thaddeus, as she'd assumed—rushed towards them.

"Stop right there!" she said, cocking her gun and ready to shoot this stranger to protect herself and David. Dressed head to foot in black, he filled out his body armour with some impressive muscles. He was not winded in the least from running. His skin was pale and if the growth of stubble was any indication he was light-haired.

"I'm with McIlroy and Preston Jones," the man said, holding his gun up and away from his body. He'd stopped running, but continued to walk towards them, taking in the messy scene in a swift glance. "My colleagues already have Thaddeus. That's why he didn't come just now. He has an impressive number of toys. He got quite annoyed when we took the flame-thrower away from him. Kept insisting he'd only just received it and had been dying to give a demonstration. He's not quite with it, is he?"

"No," David agreed, lowering his gun but not putting it away. "What took you so long?"

The blond man gave him a sour look. Glancing at his watch, he shook his head.

"I've just run almost half a mile in less than three minutes—when I got the message all the parties were present and the scene was about to go shit," he replied. Despite the curtness of his words Chelsea couldn't mistake the laughter in his tone. "I'd say it wasn't me taking my time, but rather you who didn't stall these arseholes long enough once you knew Calloway was the Boss and so-called missing link."

Chelsea looked from David to the other man, understanding that macho stupidity would have them verbally sparring and neither giving ground until one or the other broke. Losing patience, she made the decision for them, she holstered her gun, took two cable ties out of her pocket and moved over to where Phillipe writhed on the ground, clutching his leg and trying to stem the flow of blood.

"Hurts like a fucking bitch, doesn't it?" she ground out, feeling no sympathy for him. "You deserve that for leaving us to take the heat for you. There was no reason for us to separate out of the Gallery—it's in large part your fault I got shot."

"You useless fucking bitch..." he started. Knowing nothing but more venom would come from the large man, Chelsea dug a hand into her bag and pulled out a roll of tape while he continued to speak.

"I'm going to kill you, you and that arsehole you think none of us realise you're fucking every which way when our backs are turned. I should have—"

In quick motions while he ranted on, she tore off a long strip, then slapped it firmly over Kent's mouth. It gagged him perfectly. She restrained his hands and feet next, not trusting him to realise he was defeated. The movements hurt her, but she continued anyway, merely hissing in pain as the action pulled on her shoulder.

When she turned back to David and the other agent they seemed to have reached some kind of understanding. David hauled Luke to his feet and handed him over. Half a dozen more black-clad men and a few women arrived from all directions. The Agency seemed to have a handle on the mopping up of the scene.

"If we don't want to be writing reports and debriefing for the next twelve hours I suggest we disappear right now, before someone comes to ask us the first of a hundred questions," David suggested.

Chelsea glanced down at Phillipe, still writhing and trying to shout behind his gag. Looking back at David she smiled gently, the first relaxed, carefree grin she'd felt in months. Reaching out her good hand, she felt lighter just at his touch.

"Take me away?" she asked, knowing what his response would be.

"Anywhere," he replied.

Without a backward glance she let him lead her away from their captives and along the riverfront.

"Excuse me! Mr Greer, Ms Atchison? I have a Mr McIlroy on my mobile phone." The same blond man ran to catch up with them as they left the scene. "Says he's from the Dublin office and—"

They both stopped walking, turning half around so the man could catch them.

"Give me that," David said. He held out his other hand. Chelsea liked that he wasn't willing to relinquish her fingers just yet.

"You promised us three weeks," David said firmly into the phone, not letting McIlroy get a single word out. "We're taking it. As of this very moment. In a day or two—once Chelsea is well on her way to being healed and we've both had a solid twelve hours' sleep—we'll debrief to your heart's content and write a veritable thesis on the entire case. My word on it. But for now, unless the world is about to end or a nuclear holocaust is in the making, with all due respect, go fuck yourself."

"Actually, I was calling to congratulate you both and offer you the company jet to get back to Dublin with all due haste," McIlroy replied wryly. "I've called Atchison's regular doctor and she's expected for a check-up and a tetanus booster any time after lunch later today. Of course, if you're feeling that cranky then you can take my kind offer and shove it up—"

"My deepest apologies, Sir," David interjected smoothly. Feeling punchy—the morphine appeared to be wearing off—Chelsea snickered. She couldn't mistake the lilt in her man's tone, the way he caressed the words. While it felt sensual to her, she knew it was just the manner he used when sweet-talking or trying on a con. McIlroy must have heard her slightly hysterical laughter, for he urged David to have them both packed and on the plane at their earliest convenience.

"Sounds like she needs some rest and a good looking after," McIlroy finished. David flashed her that sexy grin that always made her hot. If she didn't ache in every part of her body she'd be tempted to jump him, right here and now, audience be damned.

"She'll have plenty of looking after, I'll see to that. Thank you for the jet." David hung up the phone and handed it back to the agent.

For the last time they turned their backs on the mess, and once again walked together back down the street.

"Do you think we'll know how to have a holiday?" she asked, her mind wandering.

"What do you mean?" David asked. Chelsea glanced at him, stumbled on the stoned street only to be caught by him. He wrapped an arm warmly around her waist, steadying her. This time, she focused on where she walked.

"Well, I can't remember the last holiday I had," she continued. "Particularly not one where I was completely out of contact. I've been trying to get down to the Isle of Wight, or even Brighton or the Isle of Mull for…damn, years. Do you think if we went to Fiji or something we could get away with saying our phones couldn't connect properly?"

David chuckled and pressed a kiss to her temple. Chelsea closed her eyes, loved the feel of his lips on her skin. She leaned a little heavier into his embrace, tiredness seeping into her every pore.

"I think, considering McIlroy is sending the jet, he knows exactly how this will be," he reassured her. "There will be no emergency calls, no cutting our leave short. We're heading home, and you're seeing the doctor. When you're up for it we'll fly somewhere completely isolated, have plenty of that steamy sex you promised, and let things go from there."

They came to the car. Chelsea leaned against it as David unlocked and opened the door for her. She sank into the plush seat with a sigh of sheer bliss. It felt wonderful to be off her feet. The throbbing in her shoulder continued, but no longer sent shooting pains down her arm and into her fingers.

David slid into the seat next to her and started the engine.

"I'm so glad I was partnered with you," she murmured, leaning her head back and closing her eyes. "I hate to think of having had to do this without you. We might have recovered some artsy treasures busting up this smuggling ring, but I think I'm the one who won. I ended up with you, and you're worth much more than any of that stuff."

"I'm the lucky one," David replied softly. She had to strain to hear him over the sound of the engine. "I know exactly how priceless your courage, your loyalty and your trust are. I plan to take good care of you, I swear."

She smiled, not needing to see him to know he was gazing at her with those lovely, dark eyes.

"We'll take care of each other," she reminded him.

He chuckled and agreed.

"Absolutely," was the last thing she heard before falling asleep.

In her dreams, there was only him, only them, together for always.

About the Author

Elizabeth Lapthorne has been writing professionally since 2002. She has a number of books released and is continually surprised by how much fun she has starting a new book and discovering new characters and situations that they put themselves in. She enjoys going to the gym (usually to chew over her latest problem scene), is rarely without a partially read book and has a weakness for chocolate.

Elizabeth Lapthorne loves to hear from readers. You can find her contact information, website details and author profile page at http://www.total-e-bound.com.

Total-E-Bound Publishing

www.total-e-bound.com

Take a look at our exciting range of literagasmic™
erotic romance titles and discover pure quality
at Total-E-Bound.